BI

"I don't like Gra...
live here anyway.

She laughed. "I ... ..., but I never thought of it." They both giggled.

In a second they were home again. Before, it seemed to Alice, they'd even left. She sadly looked at the lighted house and knew the evening was over. She had to go in, take off her mother's dress and shoes, and lie in bed in her room. She realized it was a lonely room, with only her usually, and whatever book she read. She liked her polka dot spread and pillow covers. She thought of them.

"What are you doing tomorrow?" he asked nervously and decided to kiss her goodnight the next date.

"What are you doing?" she answered. "I'm waiting for you." Her lips were straight when she smiled. "I was hoping you'd ask."

"Good." He was relieved because he knew he liked her.

Birdsong

James P White

METHUEN

First published in Great Britain 1985
by Methuen London Limited
11 New Fetter Lane, London EC4P 4EE
Copyright © 1977 by James P. White
Printed in Great Britain
by Richard Clay (The Chaucer Press) Ltd,
Bungay, Suffolk

British Library Cataloguing in Publication Data

White, James
Birdsong.
I. Title
813´.54[F]   PS3573.H472/

ISBN 0-413-57470-9
ISBN 0-413-57480-6 pbk

Published by arrangement with Copper Beech Press

For Janice, Edwin and Julie

CONTENTS

I.   First Love   11

II.   Solid Gold Ring   27

III.   At The Store   31

IV.   Mrs. Moody's   37

V.   Alice's Surprise   45

VI.   Amy's Thoughts   51

VII.   Dotsy At Her Trailer   53

VIII.   Sue   61

IX.   The Raise   71

X.   Alice Worries   85

XI.   Dewey Visits Dotsy   103

XII.   Lucille At Work   111

XIII.   In Alice's Backyard   117

XIV.   The Parents   123

XV.   The Wedding   137

I. FIRST LOVE

She raised her foot--put her shoe out from the desk so she could glimpse her loafers. She admired them with a proud smile. Then she looked back at the biology teacher and thought about how beautiful her shoes were.

Dewey sat behind her. He couldn't help but notice. Alice wasn't shy, looking at her new shoes. He had seldom talked with her. She was quiet and when she gave a class report, sweat popped out on her forehead. She had a habit too, of touching a shaking finger to her chin then. He would have been too embarrassed to look at a new pair of shoes of his, if anyone else were around. He was glad she did because he had often wanted to.

He looked toward Mr. Miller and he thought that he'd like to ask Alice for a date. He decided to consider it later. Alice wasn't cute; her blonde hair was too short, her complexion made him worried about his own, and she wore clean clothes that were never pretty.

The bell rang. Mr. Miller disappeared in the stir, and Dewey found himself standing in the aisle, waiting for Alice who was bent over, taking books out of her desk.

"Excuse me. I didn't see you!" she said.

"I've got all day."

"I'm sorry!" She leaned to let him pass.

"I like your shoes," he said. Like it rang a bell in his head. He really didn't. They had horseshoe buckles that made her feet big.

"They're new. Today's my birthday!" She wasn't even ashamed of telling.

"They're pretty," he said.

She thought so again as she looked down at her foot stuck out in the aisle.

"Are you sixteen?"

She nodded. "Are you?"

He couldn't believe it was the same shy girl he knew. They had been in classes for years. He had seen her a thousand times without looking and, suddenly, he felt glad just to be around her. He nodded.

"We'd better get to English. We have a test on Goldsmith."

He reluctantly followed, thinking of things he wanted to ask her.

He drove a yellow convertible polished with a caring rag. The car was rounded like the nineteen-fifties, with chrome headlights and a heavy bumper. It was no assembly-line job; it was his car, and as you slid behind the wheel, the heavy door shut quietly and the seat was soft. He could hold the convertible top switch and let the top creak back and the sky fill up the shiny car, ready to head down the road. He could see Alice was impressed when she saw his car.

He opened her car door. She was taller than he because she wore heels. Her dress made her look older.

She acted like it was privilege to get in.

He wore light blue slacks and light blue shirt and socks. His loafers were black. He was pudgy and half grown.

"I've been wishing I could see *Oklahoma!*" she said. "When you asked me, I couldn't believe it. To get asked out to eat, too!"

"Are you hungry for anything special?"

"A ham sandwich!"

"And French fries," he said, thinking of chocolate pie to surprise her for dessert.

They were leaving at five o'clock even though it was Friday because she couldn't stay out late. They sat dressed up, the top down, and were caught in the afternoon traffic of workers going home. Neither of them cared what time it was.

"I love Gordon MacRae," she said.

"I think he sings okay." He stuck his arm out for a left turn and frowned. He was jealous.

She cleared her throat. She was on pins and needles. She couldn't tell him that it was her first date.

"Do you like cars a lot?"

"They're okay."

"There are a lot of pretty new cars this year." That was almost all she knew about them. Then she remembered the book on dating that she'd read said to get a date to talk about themselves. She looked at him and forgot what she was going to say.

"Do you want the radio on?"

"Oh, yes!" She hesitated. "Do you enjoy sports?"

He nodded. "Where would you like to eat?"

"You choose. Anywhere. Do you want a ham sandwich too?"

"Yes." When he glanced at her, the breeze puffed her hair about her face. "I haven't been to Dallas on a date before," he confessed.

"Oh I haven't either. Have you ever been to the Palace Theatre?"

"Once."

"It's supposed to be beautiful."

"It is."

"Don't they have an organ that comes up from the floor and someone plays?"

He nodded.

"That's wonderful!"

He looked at her and she gazed back. They both smiled. As if the world funneled down to them, riding in his yellow car, the music soft, and their hearts pounding with fun.

They ate buttery toasted ham sandwiches at The Griddle and giggled because they had lost time finding parking space and had to hurry. The thin ham tasted good. Outside it was already dark. From the booth, they could spot the red neon Palace sign. Dewey covered the fries with ketchup to cool them, and wiped his fingers on the little cannister napkins.

"It's delicious," Alice said. "I'm so excited."

"We need to hurry."

Both of them laughed and would have rushed off if they hadn't been famished. They ate every crumb, then went out into the city street and waited in line for the show.

The movie set them into a dream, by its music and the fragile cheeks of Shirley Jones and her hair, cinched back yet tumbling down. They laughed at Gloria Graham and mused while Gordon MacRae sang "Surrey With the Fringe on Top." Walking out of the theatre, waiting for the crowd to thin, they were aware of the thick, scrolled carpeting and they were quiet.

It was breezy outside. "Wasn't that good?" Alice said, feeling like singing.

"I liked it."

They both carried parts of *Oklahoma* with them. It showed by their smiles.

"Wasn't that good?" she repeated, as they drove home. "Have you ever been to Oklahoma?"

"It isn't much."

"I never have," she said. "But I like Galveston. I was born there."

"I didn't know that."

"I've always missed the oleanders. Mother used to take me to the beach every day."

"I like Galveston," he said. "I like the waves."

"I do too, but I miss the smell of oleanders most."

"When did you move?"

"When I was three, but I remember it!" She had to laugh with him. "I really do. I'd love to live there again."

He was sure she did remember. She was one of the school brains. He never knew her to miss a single question on a test. It made him feel inferior. He missed them all the time. "I used to spend summers in Seymour," he said. "I like it."

"Do you ever think of living far away?" she asked. "Just getting far away." Somehow, the question fit her dreamy mood.

"I think of an island with a creek running through it and just me."

"I wouldn't want that. I'd like to live in China."

"I don't like Grand Prairie," he said, "but I live there anyway."

She laughed. "I don't either, but I never thought of it." They both giggled.

In a second they were home again. Before, it seemed to Alice, they'd even left. She sadly looked at the lighted house and knew the evening was over. She had to go in, take off her mother's dress and shoes, and lie in bed in her room. She realized it was a lonely room, with only her usually, and whatever book she read. She liked her polka dot spread and pillow covers. She thought of them.

"What are you doing tomorrow?" he asked nervously and decided to kiss her goodnight the next date.

"What are you doing?" she answered. "I'm waiting for you." Her lips were straight when she smiled. "I was hoping you'd ask."

"Good." He was relieved because he knew he liked her.

She was one of the class *brains*. Everyone thought anything she did was smart. They had since she was in the first grade. Whenever Alice took a test or wrote a theme, she did so with a correctness that precluded error. She could have written nothing down and been one hundred percent right.

As a result, she not only thought she was smart, everyone else did too and the teachers often didn't hunt for a possible error on her paper. They looked forward to her work. Dumber students would shake their heads and say, "She's a brain." They would have changed any answer on their paper to conform to hers. Even when they knew they were right.

But it wasn't exactly admiration. No one *wanted* a *brain* for a friend. They chose someone they could talk to. Alice often wished she wasn't a brain. She hoped to be popular. Perhaps it would have been easier if she hadn't looked smart. She had a high forehead and an aquiline nose. She was thin and her eyelashes barely showed. In her imagination, and she spent much time alone, usually reading, she pampered herself into being whoever she read about. When suddenly she realized after looking up a minute from her book, that she was after all, only Alice Cutler, then she always suffered a little disappointment.

That next night, when Dewey drove up to the house and switched off the engine, he leaned back comfortably in the car seat. He was thinking he would kiss her at the door.

"I had a good time," she said. It had been her second date. Two in a row.

He walked her to the porch and up the steps. The porch light glowed. She opened the screen, then turned to say goodbye.

"Goodbye," she said.

He stepped closer to kiss her. Just as he did, she shut the screen between them. "Oh no, you don't," she said. As if she suspected it.

He was red-cheeked, standing there, on the opposite side of the screen door. "Why not?"

"Well why should I let you?"

He hadn't thought of it that way. "Why shouldn't I kiss you?"

She came from behind the screen and sat on the steps. "I don't know why you shouldn't. I know why I shouldn't."

"Well then, why?"

"Because I don't love you."

He sat down, too, and rested each elbow on a knee. Hurt. He looked up, his hands around his chin and saw the moon over the rooftop of the house across the street. The light reflected on his car. "Why does that matter?"

"You wouldn't respect me if I kissed everybody."

"Just kiss me."

"That's how every date feels. You wouldn't respect me if I kissed you."

"But I always kiss my dates good night."

"I'm not going to be like everybody else. I'm only going to kiss the boy I'm going to marry."

He looked at the moon as he thought about what she said. "That's ridiculous," he said finally.

"Do you want to marry a girl who has kissed all her dates?"

"I *want* to kiss you."

"I *don't* want you to." She laughed.

"You can't mean that. That you're only going to kiss the man you marry. You can't see into your future."

"I'm in the present, not in the future."

He took her hand and felt her fingers tremble. "You will," he said.

She smiled, a grin. "I had fun today," she said. "More than I've almost ever had."

He wanted to kiss her hand or touch her neck. He looked at the moon. "Me, too." Already he had begun to understand her.

She was the only puritan in school and of her own free will. She went to church every Sunday because she believed in God. She listened to the sermon and at home, she often read passages of scripture to herself. Alice had simple, Christian tastes. She didn't ask her mother for clothes she didn't think they could afford. Her mother sewed plain dresses that Alice appreciated.

She wouldn't have wasted money on ice cream or bought herself a doodad or a bracelet. It wasn't that she didn't want to. She didn't think she should.

She thought she'd always rather be good than fancy.

She pictured herself an entirely different sort of girl, as a character from an English novel. It didn't matter if her notebook was cheaper than the other students'. She worried about asking for the least extra expense at school. Like club dues. She knew her parents and all of the family had to make do. She thought it was absolutely wrong not to be right.

He tried a number of tricks to get her to give him a kiss. In the movie he held her hand and thought only of it, her fingers on his, him holding her cold hand, pacing carefully when he could switch his arm around her. If he inched, she inched up until his arm rested on the back of the seat and she sat at an incline. If he swung his arm up, she would wait a second, then move it.

He never doubted that he was taken with her from that first date. As if it were a fait accompli. As if at once, he *could* love her, and the floodgates were up, the love free and from him, a natural expression. There was no love to assuage, fulfill, or conquer *him;* rather, when he loved, it showed his ability to recognize a need in him and not an aim, a need for what he loved and how he loved it, and an ability to express this need by loving. He recognized in her his own aim, or possibly, a finery in her regalia that shocked and impressed him.

"Buttercup," he would say and she turned up her eyes and wanted to laugh. "Honey, sugar, sweety, buttercup." In a row, or singly, with a whimsical note. Him tubby, nicely dressed, smiling. He would try to kiss her all the time. Nip at her cheek, her lips, her hair; want her to turn suddenly, seeing him.

"Honey, lover, buttercup."

She understood he wasn't silly. She wanted to laugh at the humor, just as he did, and their fun, and her pretended dislike of it, was only part of the humor that he would say such things, and that these phrases implied so much, yet all together, given to her as a bouquet. Like the spice of life as he said sweet things.

As if thoughtfulness were part of him, and not just his desire to please. He bought her presents he hoped she would like. He would have bought her anything and she would have been happy, but he tended to buy her a radio, a fancy doll, or a record player, to pick out just for her and give her, more than it ever would have taken to make her happy. He saw she didn't really care what he gave her. He wanted to give her even more. They were constantly together.

One Saturday morning just before Thanksgiving, Dewey woke up with a personal errand to do. He lay in his twin bed and listened to his mother running the vacuum before she left for work.

He saw the light glare on the glass covers of the prints over the other twin bed. He stretched and lay back. His closet door was shut, but the door to the back porch was open, and the bedroom was chilly. His grandmother had sewn the blue curtains and had made the matching bedspreads as well. He wasn't concerned with the curtains or the maple furniture or his shirt he had left on the floor.

People who live in accustomed homes think of routine thoughts in fragile monotonous ways that build a sense of fear and sadness. He felt both, but the brisk air--his mother had left the door open to wake him up--and the sudden decision he made, for he had been problematically thinking of it all along, cheered him up. He looked forward to the day.

"I guess you think you're going to sleep all day," his mother said, dressed for work, and powdering her face.

"I'm awake."

"I want you to mow the yard and I don't want you to gripe about it."

He didn't answer because of her tone of voice.

Both of them heard the knock and the front door open. "Oh no," his mother said, "here's Mother." She had hoped to get off early to work. "You mow the lawn," she whispered. She wore her nametag, "Lucille Sheppard" on the collar of her dress.

"Well, hello," Dewey's grandmother Dotsy said, from the front door, before either could see her. His mother frowned and sat in a chair by the closet door.

"I thought you'd be gone," Dotsy said. As if his mother weren't so fast as someone already up and visiting. "I thought I'd work in the yard."

"I cleaned the kitchen and vacuumed."

"Well I wish you'd look," Dotsy said. "A grown man lying in bed all morning."

"And he laid out till midnight."

"I got in at ten. You were up."

"Then what are you doing sleeping all day?" Dotsy and Lucille smiled.

"*I* sure haven't," Lucille said. "When I was sixteen, I didn't, either."

"Lord, none of us did. We worked from daylight to dark when I was sixteen."

"He's going to mow the yard today."

"It would have been better weather earlier this morning. It might rain."

"I don't want to get electrocuted," Dewey said.

"Isn't he smart. Getting electrocuted by a gas lawn mower." Lucille laughed and set her purse on the foot of his bed.

"*He* probably could be," Dotsy said. "After he plugged it in."

Dewey sat up and looked at both of them. "It sure is nice to sleep late." He yawned.

Dotsy looked wide-eyed at Lucille. "I think he's being smart alec," she said, grinning.

"I guess you've got a date tonight?"

Dewey didn't have to answer.

"Who is this Alice Cutler?" Dotsy asked.

"I think he's got a kingsize crush on her." Lucille glanced at Dewey.

"What do you know about it?" he asked.

"I'm your mother," Lucille said, "I know."

"I think it's sweet," Dotsy said.

Lucille smiled. "I think she's a nice girl."

"I think I'll mow the lawn." Dewey got up, holding his pajamas at the waist. They were too tight to button. He hurried to the bathroom and turned the water on full force. Then he brushed his teeth and thought about Alice himself. He was in the tub before he realized he'd get grass all over him when he mowed the lawn anyway. He sat, leaned his head against the back of the tub and looked at the steam rise from the hot bath water.

He regulated the hot water handle with his left foot, then turned on more cold with his right. He soaped his neck and face with suds.

"You mow the lawn," he heard his mother say at the bathroom door. "I'm leaving."

"Goodbye," he said, glad. He could hear from the groan of the pipes that his grandmother had turned on the patio faucet. He rinsed off quickly, dried, and put on old clothes.

"Well it's about time," Dotsy said and sprayed water at him. She watered rosebushes in the flowerbed. He hesitated, his hand still holding the screen, then he hurried to the tool shed out back where the grimy lawnmower stood.

The house inside was homey with early American furniture. The small rooms lacked a privacy none of them thought of. The living room curtains were usually drawn and the room dark, its walls sage green, the curtains orange, and brass plated plaques hung on either side of the windows. The sofa had soft arms of wide pillows. The living room was the best furnished room, the maple tables solid, the carpeting grey with a design. Just to the side was an open dining room with a maple table and five captain's chairs. When Lucille fixed up her house she usually got Dotsy to help: they sewed up curtains, never using a pattern, just taking an empty Sunday and some sale material they thought would brighten the room. Lucille cleaned with a sweat and when she got it into her head to rearrange furniture, she got Dewey and his sister Joan to help until, having put the furniture exactly alike in a hundred places, and after scouring dirt behind the sofa or under a chair, she picked one way to leave the furniture because she gave up trying. All of them thought other houses were prettier. The house lacked pretension entirely, from its white frame exterior and green shuttered windows to its asphalt roof. Dewey knew where his shoes were in the closet or the cleaner was under the sink, and whenever he wanted, he could spread his homework on the living room furniture and drink a coke as well.

He mowed the lawn while his grandmother sat in a lawn chair and watered plants. When he finished and he had yanked the hot mower back to its cranny in the shed, he bathed, and hurried off.

He took the highway to Dallas. He passed the car lots leading into town, passed the highway restaurants and the junkyards, the drive-ins and the one-story buildings that sheltered a hodgepodge of works and trades. Past the monastery on Cherry Hill and from the hill, caught a glimpse of the skyline. He drove past the miniature golf course where he and Alice had played only the afternoon before. He had thirty dollars in his pocket. Before he knew it, he was parked and there.

The shine of the jewelry store came from the clean glass counters. The polished silver gleamed, and the jewelry, arranged in velvet cases, was the object of this atmosphere. Dewey had given the matter of exactly what to buy, some thought. He stood before the cases a minute trying to locate a bracelet.

The woman beside him had her hair in a bun. "Go ahead and wait on him," she suggested to the salesman helping her. "I'm not sure."

"I want to buy a charm bracelet and a charm."

The smiling salesman took out a case of golden bracelets laid in rows.

"That's a wonderful present for someone," the woman said. "Is it for your girl friend?"

Dewey said that it was.

She lifted one easily, with her fingertips, yet it slid across her fingers. "I bought my niece one like this."

"Could I see a charm with it?" Dewey liked the bracelet. He picked out a circular charm too, with a delicate braid around the edge.

"That's lovely," she said.

The salesman nodded.

"It's what I would have chosen. You've got a lucky girl-friend to have a boy with such good taste."

Dewey followed the salesman to the cashier. The woman ducked her head over her own choice of bracelets. He passed the rows of fancy cocktail rings, then jeweled pins, and finally, watches glowing with diamonds.

"Would you like it gift-wrapped, sir?"

"Yes, please. And would you engrave it?"

"Certainly."

Dewey paid and waited a long while at the gift wrap counter. He wanted to take it to Alice at once. Hand it to her and say, "Isn't this beautiful?" then tell her it was hers. He shared her faith that someday she would be important, that the finest of anything would be in her pocket and on her face because it was in her heart. He wanted to give it to her.

He put the pink wrapped package in the glove compart-ment. For the first time, he locked it up. Then he rolled the windows up tighter because they whistled when he drove fast and the top was up and the wind rushed against them. He didn't even think of turning on the radio all the way home.

Alice sat on the floor in her bedroom and composed the last sentence of her English theme. She enjoyed writing, her paper on top the hard bench before her dresser. Occasionally she would glance at the pine oriental whatnot shelf above her bed. On it sat a tiny bamboo rickshaw her uncle Roy sent from Tokyo. She had mementoes there--a picture of her grandparents in California, her tickets to see "Oklahoma." She was at home writing on the short bench, and she enjoyed English themes. It was her spot and her world to be let out in powerful sentences of whatever she wrote. She composed them with a deliberate structure that she believed was excellent.

She finished with a wince because she had fun writing--about her favorite aunt, Willa--and she had nothing to while away the afternoon. Her mother ironed in the kitchen. Alice passed her as she went to the backyard. She glimpsed her father sitting in his chair, rustling newspaper pages. She thought he worried about his job, for when he was home he first read every word in the paper, read with his socks rolled down and his shoelaces untied, and he smoked. He couldn't always hit the ashtray as he tapped off his cigarette ashes, either. Through with the paper, he paced the narrow hall, most every night, puffing cigarette after cigarette. He smoked so that you noticed the gestures his hands and arms made, as if, when he exhaled and took the cigarette from his lips and held his hand out to balance his walk, he meant, "Well, can you beat that." No one ever doubted he thought over worries that pressured him, but no one mentioned it.

Mrs. Cutler looked up momentarily from her ironing to let Alice pass. There was an understanding between them that both were Christian. Mrs. Cutler, Amy, was a simple woman with a strong mind. She could concentrate on ironing because it was her job. Often, when she ironed, she thought of little else than the hot iron, the wrinkled material and the kitchen clock.

"Going outside?" she asked.

Alice nodded and slipped out the screen door. Into the sunny, cool day and the blue sky that swept up the flat Texas town like particles of dust. Alice didn't feel she could tell her mother anything and she didn't believe her mother would ever tell a lie.

Amy was a virtuous woman and didn't wear make-up. Sometimes, as this Saturday, she didn't take down her rolled-up hair all day; instead, she wrapped a see-through scarf around it, and saved it for Sunday church.

They joked and laughed at times. They were proud of each other--Amy of her daughter's good morals and excellent behavior (Alice had never been a problem), and Alice of her mother's good sense and too, of her mother's "talkativeness" around other people. Not that Amy talked much or to any point, but she didn't display the uneasiness Alice felt around people. Alice respected her mother as hard-working and honest. But as someone, if the need arose, she could not turn to. It would have been like missing a question on a test and asking someone who got the answer right, what it was. Her mother would have corrected her at any time, if Alice had made a mistake, and Amy would have frowned.

Alice that afternoon, under the big, free sky, sat like a bird in the swing. She hummed, out of tune. The scrubby yard, with its unkept grass and its dried up saplings, was nothing much to see. Neither were the other identical yards and houses up the block.

Yet the fantasy Alice thought grandly controlled her imagination; her feet hesitated, then pushed the swing so that the chains squeaked beneath her thin hands. She held a sense of destiny in her thoughts. She got her confidence from her belief in what she had been taught.

She looked forward to seeing Dewey at 6:30. He was her closest friend. She meant to tell him all about her aunt. She hadn't told him a million things she wanted to. That she wouldn't dare tell anyone else. Somehow, telling him was important, just as knowing about what she told was to her. In a flash, as if the sun beamed, she thought, because he likes *me*. She had to tell him this and that then, to explain why she felt a certain way about her room or about her house. To explain how she loved her mother and father and brother. Almost as if to explain it to herself. She wanted him to understand how she thought because she knew he was interested.

No one else she knew was. No one else she had ever known had been. To explain things, to tell them--such a challenge and an opportunity it offered her. His interest gave her dignity. She dreamed up a hundred things to say, fluffy, thoughtless, untrue things about herself, and then she smiled.

Such a grin, her teeth showed and her lips were alive with a discovery even before her eyes. He really does like me, she thought.

Why what could I refuse him?

In an instant it was out to herself. She did like him. More than like him. Love was no affair that carried her from reality. But then it was, he did. Oh he did, and she was high in the air, pumping the swing, with a great push, and thinking that yes, he did make her love him, and she could not wait until 6:30.

She kept her secret under tongue. When he drove up, she could have clicked it.

"Here's Dewey," her daddy said, laughing. Proud.

She saw him get out of the convertible. She sat on the polka dot bedspread. She heard him knock, come in, then she realized, as she looked into her closet and thought, "Should I wear something else," that it was important, that he did matter, that it was no longer just Dewey, but her Dewey. She realized she had nothing else to wear.

"Dewey's here," her daddy yelled.

They headed toward Dallas, both glad to see each other. Dewey wore his powder blue slacks and his blue shirt. She had never noticed the depth of his brown eyes the light blue accented.

"What did you do today?" he asked.

"The English theme. I wrote about my aunt Willa."

He bet it was good. "I want to read it." He turned the soft music on the radio lower.

"What did you do?" She wanted to sit over next to him, in his arms. She had never noticed his mouth before. He had well-shaped lips.

"I mowed the lawn." He thought of her present locked in the glove compartment. "I didn't do much of anything," he said, to catch her by surprise when he gave it to her.

"Dewey." She noticed a music in the sound of the name she had never dreamed could be there. She thought she could tell him anything and she wondered if she could tell him that she loved him. She was sixteen and she had discovered something in life that made the novels she read not only unimportant, but wrong. Inside her heart she was ringing crystal, not only showing her make-up by a high ringing, but threatening to herself to break into pieces.

"You look cute," he said. He meant that he thought she was cute. Especially with that honest grin.

"So do you."

They both laughed, and for the first time, she inched closer.

He noticed it.

She wanted to kiss his lips and hug up close against his face as they rode. For the first time in her life she didn't care what anyone else thought or said. Or about anything she knew or didn't. She wanted to kiss him, to say, "I love you."

"Come here, buttercup," he said, joking.

They were driving down Diamond Hill and it was dusk. Lit-up window lights gleamed. Spread out, like flowers, and glowing like whispers in the early dark. She scooted against him, her face on his shoulder, her lips held up, waiting for a kiss.

He kissed her gently.

"I love you," she said.

His head was absurd with love. As if she could love him. "I love you," he said and hugged her against him. For a minute the air was their breath; the lights, their eyes; the early moon, their heart.

It was forever to him. Forever to her. Without meaning to, by only saying what they felt, they opened up the serious world of life. Whatever happened was now important. Whatever they felt had not one feeling, but two. Whatever they dreamed was all they would ever want.

They sat with love a minute, startled by its importance.

Finally he spoke. "Don't you want to get married sometime?"

"Yes." She would never marry anyone else.

"Let's talk about it," he said. "About life." The vistas that opened up swallowed them as they rode along, listening to every word the other said, and thinking with their feelings, their hearts about to burst. They were new people, bound in a seriousness, aware they were in a world they never knew and only dreamed of.

"I want to do whatever you want," she said.

He thought it was right and he promised himself to take care of her as he stopped the car and proudly gave her the pink wrapped box with the golden bracelet.

II. SOLID GOLD RING

"This ring was never off my mother's finger until she died," Dotsy said. She put the gold ring into Dewey's palm. "It's solid gold; you can't buy solid gold ones anymore."

Dewey held the ring up to the light coming in the trailer window.

"You tell Alice to take good care of it. It's over sixty years old. Are you sure you want to get married?"

Dewey nodded and blushed.

"I guess you're old enough. You're out of high school. I was just fourteen when I first married and it was the smartest thing I ever did. I couldn't have found a better man. Do you remember when you lost that silver ring your daddy made you during the war?" She didn't pause; before he could have answered, she said, "I told Granddaddy that he never would find that ring--there must have been half an acre of strawberries in that patch, Dewey. And he was tired even before he started. 'It'll be dark in an hour,' I said, 'and you haven't had supper.' But he took one look at you and went right on out. Do you remember that? You went with him. I watched you two from the kitchen window while I baked cornbread."

Dewey leaned his head against the soft chairback. He slipped the wedding ring into his bluejean pocket. He listened to his grandmother talk about that night he only barely remembered. He remembered more sleeping on two large wing-backed chairs scooted together. Or before they went to bed, when he would sit on his grandfather's shoulders and peer down at the newspaper, too.

"He found it past nine o'clock and told you never to take off that ring. And you sure wouldn't, no matter who asked you to. Even when your daddy came home from the war and wanted to see it, you wouldn't take it off. You said, 'Granddaddy told me not to.' " Dotsy took a gulp of sweet iced tea. "Don never did forgive us for that, but Granddaddy never thought you wouldn't take it off for your daddy!"

Dewey didn't remember his daddy getting angry, but he still had the ring his father had made from quarters. He thought suddenly of the pictures his grandmother had, nine-

27

by-twelves of his grandfather in his casket, a rose in the suit lapel, an artificial smile on his lips. Dewey never mentioned those picutres when he turned through the endless photographs of relatives his grandmother kept in a rosewood box.

"Don was hardheaded if anyone ever was. He's the opposite of Al. Al's an easy-going guy. He doesn't say much, but no one's been better to me than he has. I'd reach down and kiss his shoe if he wanted me to."

"I hope you don't."

"You're lucky to have a stepfather as good as he is."

Dewey quit listening and thought of the hot afternoon that his father came home from the war. Dewey was six, outside playing with the garden hose, the water trinkling on his knees; when he looked down the street he saw a man in a sailor's uniform and he heard Mary, who worked in shorts and halter in her flower bed next door, call over to him that that was his daddy. Dewey ran inside and let the screen slam. "Mother," he said, and she knew, and ran outside to meet Don. When they sat in the cool living room later, Dewey watched his father kiss his mother who held the yellow covered pillow from the Philippines. The pontoon boat was a present for his older brother and an oriental doll was for his sister, and a thin large balloon was for him. He wished his father hadn't come; he wished he wouldn't kiss his mother. He had sat indoors, refusing to go outside and play, even after his daddy blew up the balloon for him.

"The smartest thing Lucille ever did was to marry Al. She doesn't have to worry now. She was poor as a churchmouse when she was married to Don."

Dewey held his tongue because he didn't want to argue about Al. He took out the ring and tried it on his little finger. The ring fit exactly. Then he reached across to the telephone on the crowded end table. The entire trailer was stuffed with memories: framed pictures of relatives, knickknacks his grandmother wouldn't give away, ivies and blooming plants in small jars and vases, embroidered pillows, and big, well-thumbed Bibles. She wore comfortable robes or plain dresses she sewed for herself. He could see the old machine in the trailer bedroom.

"This little hotbox heats up like a firecracker," she said and switched on the electric fan. "Who are you calling?"

Dewey didn't answer. He dialed the number and waited. On the third ring he heard Alice's mother say hello. "Hello," Dewey said back. "Is Alice there?"

"No, she's at the beauty shop," Mrs. Cutler said. "What are you doing calling? You aren't supposed to see the bride!"

"I'm just calling," Dewey said, embarrassed.

Dotsy listened to Dewey until he hung up. "It's always the first one that you love the most, Dewey," she said. "Papa didn't want me to marry your granddaddy and we had to sneak off to get married. I had the best man in the whole world. Nobody could have had a better husband than I did. He never said a cross word to me. I did to him, but he wouldn't fuss, he'd smile and say, "Now, Hon." If your marriage is half as happy as mine was, you'll thank the Lord and never ask him for another thing. I don't."

III. AT THE STORE

Dewey hoped, as he parked in the spaces usually reserved for customers, that his mother was in a good mood. He didn't want to have to argue about working on his wedding day. He reminded himself to pick up his shirts at Collins Cleaners across the street, put a nickel in the meter, and listened for the bell attached to the door to jingle as he walked into the store. "It's me," he told Tom who was up for the next customer.

The new store had colorful nylon sofas lined into rows, each suite with veneer end tables and shiny lamps; the chrome dinettes were set along the furthest aisle, and white porcelain electric stoves and refrigerators were plugged in and against the wall. He walked along the aisle, and looked proudly toward the front at row after row of new living room suites. He saw his mother first, and leaned on the counter where customers paid their installments.

"Look who's here!" Lucille said, seeing him at the counter. "Come on back."

Bobbie looked up from the daily cash for the Number 2 store.

"Don't you think he's too young to get married?" Lucille asked.

Dewey went into the back office and she hugged him with a show; "I do; he's still my baby." Her hair was peppered grey and black and hurriedly combed out. Her red uniform top was tight at her bust, and she wore grey framed plastic reading glasses because she had been typing. She had already changed into the thin, flat shoes she wore at work.

"I'm not your baby." He hadn't heard that in years. Despite himself, he was pleased.

"You are; you're my baby. Come back here." She kissed his cheek, and patted him on the arm. Dewey sat on one of the desks then, embarrassed.

"Lucille, can you read this?" Bobbie asked.

"Hand it here," she said. She took the pink sales slip from the Number 2 store.

"I can," Dewey said.

"I think it says '300.' You look; you've got good eyes. I can tell Clay wrote it."

"It's '500,' " Dewey said.

"That would make them 200 more short. They're one hundred short already."

"Oh, they're not!" Lucille said. "Huh? They couldn't be."

"I think they are."

"Call up Clay and ask him," Lucille said. "They'd better not be short again." Bobbie dialed and Lucille got out her powder puff. "Are you glad you're getting away from home, Dewey?" Lucille asked.

He didn't answer. He couldn't have been more glad and she knew it.

"Are you?" she asked.

"I'm ready," he said. "You want us to move in with you?"

"I sure don't!" Lucille giggled. "You were bad enough to live with! I don't even know what I'm going to wear," she said. "What's her mother wearing?"

"I don't know."

"It was 200," Bobbie said. "It still looks like 300 to me."

"Why it is 300," Lucille said. "Save it and I'll show him when he comes by." Lucille got up. "Come on, Dewey, I want to show you something." She seldom left the office except for short breaks to shop at Dayton's across the street.

Dewey followed her toward the sofas. From sweeping and dusting he knew most of the stock on the floor. When he wasn't helping deliver, he displayed the gifts for sale in the front windows, the chrome toasters, mixers, and can openers and the handblown glass ashtrays, sets of ruby glasses, and brass and copper accessories to match the popular maple furniture. Both the salesmen had customers that were interested in new living room sets. Dewey knew exactly which things he liked best in the store: which sofa and lamps and ashtrays and toasters. He liked the gifts better than the furniture because he thought that they were nicer and if he'd had a choice, he would have chosen the veneer furniture over the solid because he thought the word sounded classy.

"You don't have a sofa yet do you?" Lucille asked.

"No," he said quietly.

"Have you seen this one?"

The grey sofa had been in stock for two years. Otherwise, it was identical to the other, bright sofas. "I like it," Dewey said.

"You can have it."

He knew how excited Alice would be. "Do you mean it?"

"Yes, if you want it."

"I do." He liked it better than the aqua, red, and white sofas.

"Look over here," Lucille said. "You'll need lamps. Pick out a pair."

"It doesn't matter," he said. "Do you like those?" He pointed to a pair with blue shades he liked best.

"You don't want those for a living room. They're for a bedroom. How about the green ones?"

"They're nice."

"Well you can have them."

"I like them a lot." He couldn't keep from beaming.

"What else will you need? Let's look in the gift shop."

He hung behind, surprised that she had been so generous. He wished she'd give him the ruby glasses he liked--up close, he had noticed that two were chipped, and the pitcher had been cracked. He waited beside her and looked about the small room.

"I don't guess you need any of this, do you? Do you want any of it?"

"How about the red glasses?"

"They're too expensive!" she said. "I think they're ugly. I've got some glasses at home you can have. You don't want any of this stuff. It's overpriced anyway."

Dewey wondered when he could deliver the sofa to the small apartment on Oak that he and Alice planned to rent. He could walk to the store in ten minutes from the apartment. I wish I could take the sofa now, he thought. Then show it to Alice.

"Get the tags," Lucille said. "I've got to go back to work. Don't give them to anybody but me." She hurried to the office.

He nodded, untied the inventory tags, and hid them in his shirt pocket. Then he sat on the rubber foam grey sofa, leaned back, his head against the sofa back. He set the green lamps beside the sofa, reached up and switched them on. Often, if he were bored and had to dust, he wiped off bedroom suites in the back corner of the store and looked to see if anyone watched. If not, he would take off his shoes, lie on the sofa bed (taking off the mattress advertisement that said how comfortable it was) and perfectly relaxed, fall asleep. He couldn't doze in a chair, but curled on a good mattress or a wide sofa, he could sleep away the afternoon. Occasionally someone would wake him up and he would go back to sweeping or dusting or whatever he had grown bored of doing. When he got the chance on long dull summer afternoons though, he still napped, woke up and returned to work. Those afternoons were usually the ones that Lucille or a salesman would compliment him on how clean and polished the store was.

Dewey took Lucille the tags and she quickly stuck them in her desk drawer. "Get us a coke," she said.

He took three nickels for the machine from the coffee can by the register and bought three icy cokes that were partly frozen in the bottles. He wondered if he should ask her if he could deliver the sofa when the truck was free.

"You sure are nervous," Lucille said.

"I'm not."

"You are. Isn't he , Bobbie?"

"He looks it. I was when I got married."

"Everybody is!"

"I've got to pick up my shirts and my new suit."

"Did Number 2 come out okay?" Lucille asked Bobbie. "I'll call Clay if it doesn't."

"I'm finishing it now," Bobbie used the adding machine to check the figures.

"Here," Lucille said. She pressed two folded bills into Dewey's palm.

He put them in his pocket. "Thanks."

"Did you get all the tags?"

"Yes."

"You're going to need a raise," she whispered.

He hadn't expected a raise, too! He had never seen her so generous. "Can I have a raise?" he asked.

34

"I think you should ask Al for one. I'm sure he'd give you one if you asked him."

Dewey picked up the stapler, punched it, and dropped the folded staple into his palm. He bent it with his fingernail.

"I don't know," she said, her voice changing to a tone he clearly recognized, disappointed, even offended. "I think you owe it to him," she whispered.

He didn't want to. He glanced at Bobbie who now posted sales to open accounts. "He wouldn't give me one," Dewey said. Only two months before, when he and Alice had graduated from high school, and decided to marry as soon as possible, he asked Al if he could work at the store. Lucille told him to ask. Al had pursed his lips, hesitated, then said, "No, we don't need anyone that I can think of."

He had gone to work anyway because Lucille told him to. He helped deliver but he hated loading triple dressers, sofas, stoves, and tv's--they packed the truck and tied down the furniture, drove the bumpy city roads, delivered the furniture to housewives in plain dresses and rolled-up hair, the houses usually cramped and smelly, with excited children while the wife watched every move and warned them not to scratch anything or she'd send it back. Afterwards he and the other deliverymen stopped at cafes for pie and coffee; he listened as they flirted with the waitresses and talked about the fights. He was ill at ease, glad to return to the store and grabbed a dust rag or the vacuum or a broom and busied himself somewhere alone, or listened to Mr. Howell or Ruth sell furniture. He thought to himself then that someday after he was married he would go to college and teach school.

I won't ask Al for a raise and get turned down, Dewey decided.

"I'm asking you to ask him," Lucille said. "To show your respect."

He looked uneasily at her; both of them were suddenly angry.

"Hello Mrs. Sheppard," the customer at the counter said. "How are you?"

Lucille smiled. "I didn't see you, Vivian. I'm just fine." She looked up the account to see what the payment was.

"I'll see you later, Mother," Dewey said. "I've got to pick up my suit." When he opened the side door, sunlight glared in his eyes. He sat in his hot car a minute before turning on the ignition, then he backed out slowly. He wished he'd asked about using the truck, but he knew he couldn't have the furniture without asking for a raise.

At the stop sign he turned right, then left, and headed for Mrs. Moody's. Her house was half a block from the Baptist church. He could see the First Baptist auditorium—identical to a movie theatre, stuck on by a walkway to the rest of the church. The old yellow brick auditorium, now the chapel, had been reserved for the wedding. Across the street was a block of asphalt parking.

Sundays he used to pocket the dollar offering his mother gave him and instead have hot buttered pancakes and maple syrup at the Moody's.

IV. MRS. MOODY'S

Mrs. Moody lived in an old house that looked vacant from outside. The grass grew in patches in the shade up against the house, and needed cutting; the cracked sidewalk was unrepaired, and all the shades were drawn. Paint curled and chipped from the boards and was scraped nearly clean off the front porch.

Dewey reached the top step when, as usual, Mrs. Moody opened the door and unhooked the screen. "Well, come on in," she said. He went into the rose-papered room lighted only by two white lamps, switched on dim.

"I was just thinking of you."

Dewey followed her into the bright kitchen; she turned down the fire under a covered iron pot. "Phyll's gone out to pick up your wedding present. I was just thinking how much you'd like some of this spaghetti."

"I didn't come for lunch." He tightened the cap on the finger nail polish bottle that sat near the salt shaker. He loved her spaghetti. She had said that basil was her secret to making real Italian sauce.

"It's going to be delicious. You'd better have some." She carefully took a single bay leaf, raised the heavy top, her potholder in her hand, and with steam swirling out, dropped in the leaf and returned the lid. "I know."

"If you have enough, " he said, unable to resist the tempting smell.

She took the pot off the burner and let the bay leaf flavor the pungent sauce. "I thought so," she said.

Mrs. Moody had a wise face that showed her confidence in what she thought. She could convince Dewey of something simply by her intonation, because her voice displayed the same self-confidence--not, however, in what everyone else believed in. He thought that she was one, possibly the only adult in town who thought for herself. She didn't like the look-alike houses of Golden Brook Homes or the food at the cafeteria everyone ate at after Sunday church, or, for that matter, the people themselves. And she had spent all her life in Grand Prairie.

She didn't account for *why* people in town were so provincial (she certainly didn't know other than that their *parents* were); she accounted for *how* they were and agreed with him, but never attempted to answer his "but *why* are they?" "Why shouldn't they be?" she'd ask back.

He knew that she disliked what he disliked so he listened carefully to what she did like and none of it was in Grand Prairie, except for the rare, rainy days when the sky darkened and the streets and yards flooded. She sat inside, her front door closed, and she said that Mexico City was the most beautiful city in the world, and Taxco had the finest silver, and that no one--no white person--could live in Mexico without a maid, although she was afraid that hers, Juanita, had once brought her a dish of fried dog. It had tasted delicious, but afterwards, sitting on the sofa in her living room, she ruminated over Juanita's comments and thought that perhaps the "pero" in the name of the dish--one of those unpronounceable Spanish names and she never learned Spanish--meant "dog." "Then," she said, "the aftertaste was dreadful."

"I should have heard from 'Father,' " she said, referring to her husband. "He's in Albuquerque this month. I'm going to tell him to bring me some of those polished stones and I'll give you one. They're rocks that have been handcrafted until their lucent. They're every bit as nice as precious stones. The American Indian had a culture that we haven't recognized after two hundred years. I never have seen what is so beautiful about a diamond."

"They're expensive," Dewey said.

"Well why are they? I wouldn't want to wear something that someone would cut my finger off to get. The best dressed, most beautiful women in the world are in Mexico City and they wear--turquoise."

"I wish we could go there for our honeymoon," Dewey said.

"You can go with us the next time we go."

Dewey wondered what Phyllis was buying for him and Alice. He looked at the framed photographs on the kitchen wall--black framed photos of horses with flowers over their saddles and beside the strong horses with raised heads, was either Mr. Moody alone with the smiling jockey, holding the reins or the group of them: Mr. and Mrs. Moody, Phyllis, and Paul.

He was fascinated by those photographs. The horses' names: Miss Phyll, Deliver, Prince of Sasha, were printed in ink across the top, along with the size of the purse: $1500, $1250, even $2500. Mrs. Moody was only in one photo and she looked younger, but worn out. It was a night race and Dewey thought that she must have gone because they stayed at what she called a one-horse hotel, an old hotel with a bath at the end of the hall, no air-conditioning, the window open and her fanning, complaining, and sending her son Paul for food to go, food brought in cardboard containers wrapped with string and set on the dresser, the bureau, the window sill. If she liked the room, she stayed in it, let the others go while she read, or simply thought (she didn't have to read all the time), but if the crowded room was hot, she went to the races, and occasionally, he guessed from the photo, would pose at the winner's circle too. She had said that usually, winning nights, they ate large Chinese dinners because it was her favorite food.

The photographs showed Phyllis in pigtails, and Paul then hardly to Phyll's waist, and Mr. Moody. Dewey had never been to a horse race, much less to Mexico; he was always fascinated by the jerseys and the horses and the glimpses of the track, and surprised that the Moodys had won those purses. He thought they should have been rich. "You should go with us next time," she had told him before, but he had always worked and sometimes Mr. Moody came home for a week instead of having them travel to him.

She set down the plate of spaghetti on the red and white checkered cloth. "Do you want iced tea or milk?" She fixed sweet tea for them both and sat across from him.

"It's good," Dewey said.

"Of course it is--the recipe is from my grandmother." Mrs. Moody's smile was flat, even; she smiled only with her lips and her bright narrow eyes. "I won't even give you the recipe, so don't ask. But I'll give it to Alice if she promises not to tell a soul. It's a family recipe."

"You have to tell Alice."

"I'll tell Alice so she can fix it for you. And I'll give her my potato salad recipe. I put dill in it. Dill makes all the difference in the world."

"I was at the store this morning," Dewey said, "and Mother gave me a sofa and lamps."

"What color is it?"

"Grey. But I have to ask Al for a raise."

"Why?"

"In order to get the sofa."

"I don't see why," Mrs. Moody said.

"Because Mother wants me to – but he'll just say no. He doesn't even want me to work at the store."

"Well, why not?"

They heard the front door open and understood it was Phyll. She carried a large white wrapped box with a white satin bow. "I saw your car outside, Dewey boy," she said. Her smooth black hair hung to her shoulders; she wore horn-rimmed glasses that made her look intelligent. He had thought she was smart when he first saw her because her glasses were so thick.

"What is it?"

"That's a surprise."

"What is it, Phyll?"

"Nick and I bought it last night. Alice said you needed it."

"Look here," Dewey said, pointing to the picture of Phyll in pigtails. "Wear your hair like that tonight."

"Is your suit ready, Phyll?" Mrs. Moody asked. "You can't be late."

"No-o," she said, hurrying out. Phyllis went into her old room which Mrs. Moody had partly converted to a sewing room. It was the nicest room, with thick, brown carpet, a fine pecan bed, and in the corner, the used electric sewing machine under a metal pole lamp. Although there were five rooms in the house, not counting the backporch, the family only gathered in three: the living room, the kitchen, and Phyll's. The other two were private. Paul's was unkept--one of his metal twin beds was used for dirty clothes--and Mrs. Moody's was empty except for her plain double bed and the small dresser and mirror. Her room didn't have carpet or curtains, just closed venetian blinds and bare hardwood floor. Dewey had seen it once, looked in when everyone else was in the kitchen and had hurried back to them.

"I've got to go back to the store," Dewey said.

"Are you going to ask for the raise?"

"Do you think I should?" he asked.

"I don't think you have to."

"I do. Mother's trying to make me say 'thank you' to Al."

"Is asking for a raise saying thank you?"

"Yes, because I have to ask."

"But you don't have to. You're almost a married man. I bet you'd be surprised how your mother would act if you *didn't* do what she wanted."

Dewey considered the idea. He thought it wouldn't work, no matter how it sounded. If he didn't ask, he wouldn't get the furniture. "You don't know her," he said.

"I've known her for ten years."

"You couldn't possibly know her without living with her," he said. "You can't believe what she says."

"Then maybe she doesn't want you to ask for a raise."

"You can believe that she does." He could see that he had to decide for himself. He thought Mrs. Moody was smart but she couldn't understand the situation. He didn't think his mother did, either. He couldn't see any solution except swallowing his pride and asking Al for the raise. "If I have kids," he said, "I'm not going to try to make them unhappy."

"They'll be unhappy anyway," Mrs. Moody said.

"But they won't be so frustrated. I'll try to help solve their problems, not make them. When you're forty you ought to be able to help people who are young. I could help a six-year old."

"But when you get older you get too many problems for yourself," Mrs. Moody said. "You're the happiest you'll ever be right now."

"That couldn't be true."

"Well it is. Do you think that I ever wanted to live in Grand Prairie? Or live in this old house?"

But you look happy, he started to say. You do as you please. No one bosses you. Then he thought of her waiting for the check, of the old house that was, if you looked at it, falling down, or Mr. Moody at some racetrack and of Mrs. Moody at home, with no place to go that she wanted, shut up inside with books and whoever dropped in. He thought he'd rather die. He thought he'd rather have his own problems. Maybe she was right. "Yes," he said, "you woudln't live anywhere else."

"I sure would!"

The phone rang and her face brightened. "I bet that's Father," she said. "He must have gone on to Denver."

"Phyllis," Dewey called out.

"Umhmmm."

"Don't you be late tonight."

"I'll be there about ten," she said, "after the wedding."

Dewey got up, and passed Mrs. Moody on the phone. He picked up the big white present.

"It was a wrong number," she said, hanging up the receiver.

"That's the best spaghetti I ever ate," he said.

"I told you it would be. Tell Alice I'll give her the recipe." She took the plate to the sink and turned on the faucet. "Are you going to ask for the raise?"

"I don't know," he said. He wanted to ask her again if he should. "I guess there's no way to tell. He sat in a chair in the corner of the living room. "I don't want to," he said.

"Why you don't really need it. I bet Alice doesn't care about money. She's not that kind. She's one of the finest girls I know."

"I care," he said. "I want the furniture."

"Then ask him. You can't make a mistake by asking."

He sat quietly a minute. He looked about the high-ceilinged room where he had spent many afternoons talking with her. He felt perfectly relaxed. He thought that her furniture wasn't new and he asked himself why should his be. For no reason he wanted the new furniture more than ever. "I don't know," he said.

"You don't have to," she said. "No one can make you."

"But I want it." He was embarrassed and felt greedy.

"Then ask and don't worry. I bet your mother wants to give you the raise and the furniture. Otherwise she wouldn't have brought it up."

Dewey thought about what she said. "Can you believe I'm getting married today?" he asked.

"I don't know why not."

He liked that. He sat back and he sniffed the pungent sauce. "You sure are a good cook," he said. "The best I know."

"Anytime you want spaghetti you tell me boy," she said.

"Thanks for the present," he called to Phyll before he left.

Mrs. Moody followed him to the door. She always did. Dewey looked familiarly at the comfortable sofa, the inevitable newspaper folded, waiting to be reread, the hand mirror on the side table, beside the lamp base. He listened for her to say it. He stepped onto the porch.

"You come back soon, boy."

"I will, bye." As he walked to the car, he smiled. He liked to hear her "come back soon" that she always made a point to say. She said it every time, and he worried that if she didn't, she didn't want him to come back. He waved, as he drove off, and unexpectedly said 'bye bye' aloud, although no one could hear him.

V. ALICE'S SURPRISE

Alice took one of the square slips from the paper bag and unfolded it. She read it twice first.

"Read it aloud, Alice," Mrs. Clapper said.

"Don't go to bed mad," Alice said.

"That's the best advice you'll get. Talk any problem over before you go to sleep. Otherwise it will be worse in the morning."

"Why didn't I think of that?" Mrs. Wyatt said. "Mine's silly. You'll know it when you get to it."

"I couldn't think of anything," Agnes Stard said. "I wrote down one word."

Alice blushed deeper and drew out another slip. She'd planned to spend the morning in the tub when her mother asked her to go next door for boxes to store her things in. She had knocked on the back porch, and Mrs. Clapper took her through the wallpapered hallway into the living room of presents and neighbors and her mother, who had crossed the yard around front. Presents were stacked on the black tv.

She read the next slip: "Have children."

She knew Mrs. Clapper didn't write it because she didn't have any. Alice liked this advice best. She thought her mother wrote it.

"But think twice first," Brodine said. "They'll break your heart every time."

"They sure will," Agnes said. "Even more the older they get."

Mine won't, Alice thought, and read more advice: "Wear perfume at 5." She was aware of her rolled-up hair and a rash of nervous pimples on her face. She didn't look up.

"Don't meet your husband at supper in a housecoat," Mrs. Hyatt said. "I think it's awful for a wife to spend the day in her robe. I always put on perfume at five o'clock."

"You put on perfume?" Agnes said. "After I've cooked and cleaned all day, Nate had better take me just how I look. He's more interested in how his supper looks than how I do. I wish you could see what *he* looks like when he gets home."

"I didn't mean look fancy. I just think a woman should fix up."

"Well, read another one," Mrs. Clapper said. "We're all learning something."

"I always wondered what I did wrong," Bobbie said. "Now I'm going to find out. But I had children and I fixed up."

"You must have gone to bed mad," Agnes said.

"We got to where we never went to bed," she said.

Alice was red with embarrassment, but couldn't help and laughed with the others. She didn't think she needed advice. She glanced at the stack of presents and thought how glad she was to have them. Her brother Jonathan was shaking them early to guess what was inside.

"Read another one, Alice," Agnes said. "You haven't come to mine."

"I think we should have done this before *we* got married," Mrs. Clapper said. "I hope you appreciate this good advice, Alice. What did you write, Amy?"

Amy just smiled.

"Well you won't have any problems, Alice," Mrs. Clapper said. "I've never heard you disagree with anyone. If you don't argue with anyone they won't argue with you."

"Unless they're hungry and you don't have supper ready," Agnes said.

"Be neat." Alice read it louder than the others. For a minute, no one said anything. Then Alice said to herself, that's mother's. She recognized the lopsided handwriting.

"That's always good advice," Bobbie said. "My husband gave it to me every time he came home."

Alice glanced at her mother who looked away, toward Jonathan. I am neat, Alice thought.

"Cleanliness is next to godliness," Mrs. Wyatt said. "A clean house is important."

"Church," Alice read. Bobbie giggled. "That means go to church."

"Don't go to bed mad, is best," Mrs. Clapper said. "If you'll talk it over first, you won't wake up mad. You tell Dewey that. Open your presents, Alice. Amy said you haven't even packed yet."

"Okay." Jonathan brought them, stacked on the big rectangular bottom one, and Alice felt like it was Christmas. She unwrapped a stiff white bow, and in the box, was a glazed pottery plate with a hand painted picture of Mrs. Clapper's red cow on her farm. The cow stood up to its knees in blue-bonnets.

"That's from me," Bobbie said. "I painted it and if you look close some of the features are like Edna's because she kept getting in front of the cow."

Alice read the inscription on the back: Dewey and Alice, *June 12, 1962.* "Thank you," Alice said.

"You should wear glasses when you paint," Edna said. "Alice, you can store that in your mother's garage."

Alice pulled on the satiny red string wrapped around the next box. "They're beautiful," she said. The embroidered cup-towels were simple designs of flowers.

"Thank you," Agnes said. "Everyone can always use cup-towels."

She got a blue glass ashtray and a set of clear salt and pepper shakers and six linen napkins. Then she shook the largest box. The card read: "from the neighbors." "We all chipped in," Mrs. Clapper said. "If you don't like it, you can exchange it for something else."

Alice could tell it was wrapped at a department store. Past the thick white wrapping she touched folds of tissue, then the softest green blanket she had ever seen.

"Everyone can use another blanket," Mrs. Clapper said.

"Thank you," Alice said. Her face made the blanket like Christmas.

It was nearly eleven.

"Alice," Amy called.

"Yes?" Alice was packing her suitcase for the honeymoon. She had carefully folded her new white pleated skirt. When her mother didn't answer, Alice went into her parents' bedroom. "Yes?"

Their bedroom hadn't changed in the fifteen years they'd lived in it: the old dresser with the cosmetics kept in the drawers that stuck, the little cup her mother kept bobby pins in, the hairbrush and black comb, the shaky, floral covered dresser bench. On one side of the dresser was a picture of Alice, seven and smiling, one tooth missing and her hair in curls; on the other side was a photograph of her baby brother when he was fat and just beginning to sit up. The hardwood floors were waxed and clean. Although the house was small, Alice only went into her mother's room to borrow something to wear or to use the magnifying mirror her mother kept in a bureau drawer. The room was always unfamiliar to her.

"I want to talk with you. I want to show you something," she said and went into the small, hot bathroom, the medicine cabinet mirror still cloudy, drops of water running down it. Alice's brother had just bathed. In the winter the bathroom was hot from the sweet gas wall burner, and in summers the bathroom was hotter, even with the window open and the shade up: the mirror fogged and the towels got damp and anyone bathing, sweated and was glad to dry off and get out.

Amy opened the towel cabinet, moved the front towels, each white with faded printed flowers, and took out from beneath the back rows of towels, a hidden round plastic bag she unsnapped.

Alice couldn't see what she took out, but she understood the rubber bag inside was a douche bag. She said nothing because her mother didn't.

"You'll probably want to get a diaphragm," Amy said, opening her palm. "Men don't like to use anything and you'll have to."

Alice thought it looked uncomfortable.

"Here," Amy showed it to her. When Amy was authoritative she wasn't embarrassed. "You'll have to go to the doctor to get one fitted, but it isn't expensive."

"I went to Dr. Banks. He's real good," Amy said. "I thought you should know what's best to use. I don't like creams."

Creams sounded acidic. Why use anything, Alice thought. Dewey won't want me to. But she looked closely at what her mother showed her.

"I wouldn't use the pills until they're tested more."

"No," Alice said.

"It isn't embarrassing," Amy said. "The doctor will be in just as much of a hurry as you."

"Oh," Alice said, blushing.

"I just wanted to tell you," Amy said.

"I'm glad," Alice said and went into the bedroom. She sat down and breathed, like she'd been holding her breath. She was as red as a lobster. She sat on her bed and listened to her mother put back the towels. When she heard her mother come into her room, she pretended to be packing the suitcase.

"Do you need any help?" Amy's voice had changed back: high, confident, excited Alice was getting married.

"I don't think so," Alice said.

"I like that slip," Amy said. Alice had bought the new pink slip to wear with her wedding suit.

The room was a mess of cosmetics and new and old clothes, dresses Alice hadn't decided whether or not to take on the honeymoon, and powders, eye make-up, lipstick, and hairspray on the dresser and headboard.

"You need to clean out the bureau too," Amy said.

"Why?"

"I told Jonathan he could have your room. I'm going to make his into a sewing room."

"What should I do with everything?"

"There are some boxes in the garage. You can leave them there. I'll help after I finish cleaning." Amy sounded like she meant spring cleaning but she didn't.

Alice didn't pack anything for a while. She was used to her room. She didn't want it empty. She thought her brother was selfish to ask for it. It was part of her and the family. When it's Jonathan's, she thought, we won't have my room to stay in. She saw her little brother at the doorway; he wore his Indian suit and feather headdress Amy had made.

"Would you bring me some empty boxes from the garage?"

"I'm going outside," he said. "Can I look at your presents first?"

"If you get me some boxes you can." She knew he wouldn't when she asked, but she tried to make him feel guilty for being lazy. He never did what anyone asked him to do, even her daddy.

49

Alice could get angry at him for the slightest thing. She thought someone should make him mind. She thought her daddy should, but he only made excuses for him. "He's still a boy," her daddy said whenever Alice told on him. When he'd taken an afternoon paper route that past year, Amy had ended up throwing the papers all week because Jonathan had gone out to play and hadn't come home when she told him. To punish him, Ed took away his paper route.

"You can't have my room if you don't get the boxes," Alice said.

"It's not your room any more; you're getting married."

"It's mine as long as I'm here."

"It's mine as long as I'm here," Jonathan mimicked.

"It is," Alice said.

He said nothing and Alice turned away, her lips tight. She wanted to slap him. When she looked again, he was gone, and she wished she hadn't argued. She had meant to be especially nice to him, to give him a billfold she'd bought. He should have gotten them, she thought. She wondered if her mother had heard and she felt embarrassed. I'll get the boxes; I don't mind, she thought. She sort of wanted to rummage in the garage.

Alice turned back to the clothes, still on hangers, that she had piled on the bed. She noticed an old dress she'd had since her freshman year in high school. She thought she'd thrown it away. The dress had a big circle skirt, with a bolder plaid than Amy liked. The black blouse top was shiny from washing and ironing.

She put it in a new pile and decided she would give some of the clothes away. Amy would want a couple of them for quilts. She thought how warm the green blanket would be on a cold night.

Then she went back into the bathroom and pushed the lock on the door. She turned on the water in the sink, took out a fresh wash rag and her acne soap. She dug behind the towels in the cupboard and took out the sack her mother hid. She could hear the radio on in the kitchen. She opened the plastic box with the diaphragm and looked at it a minute. Then she put it back, and hid the plastic sack. The radio still played. She wiped perspiration off her face and sat on the pink chenille commode top. She could not even tell Dewey how excited she was.

VI. AMY'S THOUGHTS

Amy had seen Alice, her feet on top of her bed, boxes of souvenirs and clothes surrounding her. Alice had kept all her letters, souvenirs from vacations, dried corsages, ticket stubs, photographs of friends and teachers, even scarves she'd especially liked. They were in pink stationery boxes, small brown cardboard boxes, weak white flower boxes.

The room was inside out, the drawers emptied, their contents not yet packed because as Alice said, she wasn't sure where she wanted to put what. She hesitated to leave it anywhere it might get lost again. "I can't take all this with me," she told Amy. Her two red suitcases were both small.

"You don't have to," Amy said. "It'll be safe in the garage."

Amy had glanced at the old black blouse dress Alice had out on the bed.

She went into the kitchen and turned on the radio. She sat at the dinette and looked at photos she had found--under her dresser drawer. The photos were of Galveston where Alice was born.

When she and Ed had first married, they had joined the Young People's Training Union of the First Baptist Church. Their apartment was in an old house on Wall Street, and Ed had a job with the Army. He had learned engineering in a CCC camp and didn't have a college education. He went to flying school for a pilot's license and studied radio and electronics at the YMCA.

They used the outside stairs to their apartment. The apartment faced the alley. She had shopped at a grocery a block and a half away, walked along the alley, then up the wooden steps. She was tickled that Mrs. Malone who lived downstairs and was eighty-two, told her over and over what a cute family they were. Mrs. Malone brought little presents that continually surprised her.

She had disliked the Gulf Coast humidity. Ed had too; he sweated, bent over the car engine weekends, and at night he stretched on the sofa while she used a hot washrag to pick the pimples on his back. But he had looked good: lots of curly hair and he smiled a lot.

Their first weekend in Galveston she had gone to Mutual Life about a secretarial job, but had been told that married women weren't hired.

She cooked cornbread every night because Ed liked it. She knew she was lucky: she won a freezer from Montgomery Wards and just before they left Galveston, she won a refrigerator in another contest, and sold her old icebox for five dollars.

Amy saw Alice walk down the narrow hall to the bathroom. She went into the living room then and sat in her favorite chair by an open window. She felt cooler and she waited a minute.

In less than a day Alice would be gone--she knew how quickly--soon Jonathan would be, too. Amy dug her finger into the ivy plant on the table; the soil needed watering.

She hated for her family to start breaking up. Outside, through the slant of blind she raised, Mrs. Wyatt passed by in her new brown Chevrolet. The car lurched whenever she let out the clutch.

Amy listened to the water running. She had never told Alice that she was not the oldest. She never told anyone when she thought of her baby that had died. She hadn't seen Robert's grave since they'd left Galveston, but he was her first, two years older than Alice, and was buried in a small grave in a cemetery near Wall Street. She hadn't even thought of him in over a year. She wished she could see Galveston.

It seemed to her that she and Ed hadn't been married long. Like she should be able to push Alice in her carriage the half-mile to the seawall. She remembered as clear as a bell when she was Alice's age. She had finally agreed to move to Galveston. Ed had to go. She thought about telling everyone bye a long time afterwards. And the humidity had made her sick most of the year.

She heard a car pull up in the driveway. When she looked out, she was surprised.

VII. DOTSY AT HER TRAILER

Dotsy's trailer got hotter every morning after 8, and by the time Dewey left, she had the fan on medium. She dialed first her daughter Maxine who wasn't home, then told her daughter Irene that she'd given Dewey the ring. "I think that's wonderful," Irene said. "You tell him to come by here today. Maxine and Paula are shopping," she said. "They're coming by your place later. I want to give Dewey a hug."

"Well his eyes were as big as saucers," Dotsy said. "I sure do love him."

"I do, too," Irene said. "I'll call Lucy. Let me hang up now."

Dotsy put on sauerkraut, then went outside, watered the canteloupe, and sprayed the squash she had planted alongside the trailer. She washed Stars because he had lost his flea collar, and she listened for the mail. Hoped it would come early.

She was watering when Maxine and Paula drove up. "Come on in," she said. "I sure am glad to see you."

"Let's go inside," Maxine said. "You've got the grass soaked. Come on, Paula."

They sat in the living room, and Dotsy turned the fan on high. "Do you like these Mexican sandals?" she asked. "I wish you'd bring me a pan next time you go."

"I will," Maxine said. "I didn't know you wanted any. Look here Paula," she said, handing her a snapshot of when Paula was 8.

"Dewey had that out," Dotsy said. "He sure does love to go through those old pictures."

"Isn't that a pretty ashtray," Maxine said. "Where did you get it, Mother?"

"Lord, that's not an ashtray. I got that dish at a Mormon rummage sale in Fort Worth. You were with me," Dotsy said.

"No, I wasn't with you. Was I?" Maxine combed through her short, wet hair, helping it dry.

"I thought you were. If you weren't, you sure didn't miss anything. Do you want it?"

"I'll take it," Paula said. She wasn't pretty; she had big hips like her mother, and her face was too full, especially with her white round glasses.

"What are you going to do with it? You haven't started smoking have you?" Dotsy asked.

"No, I haven't. But Butch smokes."

"I'm giving it to you, not to Butch. I don't like that nasty stuff. I wouldn't let a boyfriend of mine smoke."

"I thought it wasn't an ashtray," Maxine said.

"It isn't, unless Paula's going to use it for one. I just set it there because I thought it was pretty."

"I think it's pretty; that's why I asked you where you got it. Peweee--doesn't that sauerkraut stink."

"You don't have to eat any. Here, Paula," Dotsy said, "go ahead and take it honey, I don't want it."

"Thank you." Paula sat with the purple dish in her lap. Her smile left as fast as it had come; she sat back in the wide chair, her arms around her waist.

"But I don't know, Mother," Maxine said, "I was younger than Dewey when I got married."

"You're a woman, Maxine. That makes a difference."

"Does it? What difference does it make? I went to work just like Clarence did."

"A man should be out on his own before he gets married. Otherwise he might not know what he wants."

Maxine laid the comb on the table and felt the ends of her hair. "It's still wet, Paula," she said, then turned to Dotsy. "Clarence knew what he wanted. We've been married twenty-five years."

"But did he know what he was getting?" Dotsy said.

"I guess he did if he's stayed with it this long," Paula said. "I'm going to choose my husband, he's not going to choose me."

"You better tell Butch that. I thought you'd already chosen."

"Maybe I have," Paula said, "and maybe I haven't. I'm sure not going to tell him."

"I never had a doubt the minute I saw mine," Dotsy said, "and neither did he. I didn't tell him right off, either, Paula. I couldn't have gotten a better man. I wasn't at his beck and call like some of these women and he didn't want me to be."

"I don't think Dewey's too young. He's got a good job down at the store. I wish I could meet Alice. I told Dewey to bring her by the house, but he hasn't. Is she pretty, Mother? Paula, feel my hair. Is it dry enough?" Paula felt the short hair. They both had just cut their hair and the stringy haircut showed their short, wide necks. Maxine didn't need glasses, but she had the puffy cheeks, only more wrinkled, and high moon eyebrows that looked painted on. She wore a blue and white striped muu-muu like Paula's red. "It's still wet," Paula said.

Dotsy flattened her lips together. "Lord no, Alice isn't pretty."

"I heard she doesn't talk much."

"She doesn't say a word. I don't know what he sees in her, but if I ever saw a guy hooked, he is. He was mooning around here this morning."

"Mrs. Porter said that Alice went with her mother to football games until Dewey asked her out," Maxine said. "She told me Alice made the best grades in school but she didn't know anything about boys."

"That's old gossip," Dotsy said. "She's friends with Alice's mother." Dotsy leaned up, to see out the trailer window. "Is that the mail?"

"I don't see anybody. Are you expecting something?"

"No, I'm not."

"Why would Dewey want her?" Paula asked.

"Lord, I sure don't know what he sees in her," Dotsy said. "But he was as happy to get Mother's ring as any boy in the world."

"What ring?" Maxine asked.

"I let Alice have Mother's. It was never off her finger while she was alive."

"Do you mean Grandma's wedding ring? I wanted that ring for Paula."

"Oh no!" Dotsy said. "Why didn't you say something?"

"Because I didn't know you were giving it away. I told Paula a year ago that if she married Butch, she could have that ring."

"She did," Paula said. "She sure did."

"Well I wish I'd known it."

Maxine pooched out her lips. She got a hard, shiny look in her eyes. She didn't speak for a minute and Dotsy waited, wishing she knew what to say. She could see Maxine had flown off the handle.

"Well we've got to go. Come on, Paula," Maxine said and got up. She motioned for Paula to leave the plate.

"There's no need to be mad," Dotsy said and got up too, the three of them crowded standing in the small trailer living room for the furniture was large and covered with pillows Dotsy made. Dotsy noticed a spot on the white lace doily under the lamp and wondered what it was, and she frowned, watched Maxine unfasten the hook lock on the screen door, and say, "I'm not mad," push the door open and step onto the front porch which had a white picket gate to keep Stars in. You sure are, Dotsy thought.

"Don't you want this plate?" Dotsy held it out to Paula, but Paula was opening the car door--shook her hands because the door handle was hot--and sat inside, fanning, rolling down the window. Dotsy watched them drive off. "Oh no," she said to Stars.

She hurried to the soft daybed, sat on top the quilt and picked up the telephone. She could dial without her glasses because she used the telephone a lot.

Dotsy saw the mailman put a letter in her box just as the phone rang. "Lucille," she said. She had half a mind to hang up and get the letter.

"Hello," Lucille answered.

"I'm in hot water again," Dotsy said. "Maxine just left mad as a hornet."

"What happened?"

"She and Paula weren't here five minutes before she blew up. I just mentioned that Dewey came by this morning for the ring. You should have seen how thrilled he was to get it. He sure did want it. Bless his heart."

"I know he did."

"Well I thought it was cute. He was dressed to a T--even had his shoes shined. I hope he makes it through the day without a heart attack."

"He is nervous. He's nervous as he can be. He came by here trying to fuss."

"You'd have thought I'd hit Maxine in the face when I told her. She said I promised her not you the ring. I told her I hadn't promised anyone the ring."

"You didn't promise me the ring."

"I did say I'd give it to the first grandchild that got married. You were right here in this trailer when I said it. But Bill was first and didn't want it. I sure was glad because his wife thought she was too good for a gold band. I'd rather have one, any day."

"I never told Maxine you promised me the ring."

"I never did. I never promised it to anyone. I was fixing sauerkraut for lunch and she kept holding her nose, making fun. Beggars can't be choosers, I say, but I ignored her ignorance. I gave Paula that little blue ashtray I got in Fort Worth. I thought everything was just fine until I mentioned Dewey. Maxine did say that Dewey wouldn't bring Alice by to meet her. I don't blame her for wanting to meet Alice."

"I don't either," Lucille said. "They brought Butch by to meet me. I appreciated it."

"But I bet Paula doesn't marry Butch anyway--she just wants to get attention for herself. She wouldn't even tell me goodbye. She'd be lucky to get him."

"What'd you tell Maxine, Mother?"

"She wouldn't let me tell her anything. You can't fuss with her, she just takes off. I haven't forgotten how she acted the last time I was in Arizona. When I was sick at Earl's--I mean sick, flat on my back with the flu, and she got mad because I wouldn't stay with her right then. You remember, Lucille, how crowded they were when she was decorating sunglasses with rhinestones. She worked for that Mr. Darrell."

"I remember."

"She had rhinestones all over the carpet of that house-- like it had rained rhinestones. I bet there were six million. She and Paula were trying to get them all up because she was going to sell the house, and she wanted me there to help them. I told her I didn't feel like helping them and she said 'What in the hell did you come out here for if you aren't going to stay

57

with your own daughter?' I haven't forgotten it. I've never held it against her, but I don't appreciate it." Dotsy swallowed. "Lucille?"

She heard the receiver scrape against something hard, then heard Lucille say, "I was just handing Ruth an invoice."

"I don't know what to do. She's not going to be happy as long as Dewey has that ring."

"Well, why did you give it to him?" Lucille asked. "Just a minute, I've got to go to the register."

Dotsy waited. "Get away from there, Stars." She nudged the dog with her bare toe. Stars licked again at her foot, and Dotsy wiggled her toes, and held her foot against her calf. "I guess Maxine's mad at us, Stars." She listened to the office talk but couldn't understand. "Hurry up," she said into the phone.

"I'm back," Lucille said.

"I'm not going to call her," Dotsy said. "Not when she comes to my house and acts like that. I don't hold my nose at her house."

"I wouldn't call her either," Lucille said.

"Do you think Dewey really wants the ring? I don't think Paula is going to be happy until she gets it."

"I don't think they've got the money for a ring," Lucille said. "That's why he was so glad to get it."

"Poor old Dewey," Dotsy said. "His eyes were as big as saucers when I handed him that ring. They had to cut it off Mama's finger after she died, did you know that?"

"No. I didn't much want to know it."

"They had to because her fingers were so swollen. She wouldn't let anyone take it off while she was alive."

"Just a minute," Lucille said, and put the phone on 'hold.' Dotsy's ear hurt from the noise.

"I'd have hung up," she told Stars, "if I'd known she was going to do that." She looked out at the mailbox. "I believe that's Maxine," she said, and hung up the phone, just as the white Ford parked in front of the trailer. She watched Maxine hurry out, her short straight hair flying. "Come on in," Dotsy said, "I hated to see you run off like that."

"Paula forgot her dish," Maxine said. She leaned against the arm chair and brushed her skirt smooth. "Um ummm, doesn't that sauerkraut smell good."

"Tell Paula to come in and let's have a plate. I've got the weiners ready to boil." Dotsy got up from the sofa. She had the bright blue plates already out and waiting.

"We can't stay. This dish is pretty, isn't it. Made in Japan."

"Does it say that?" She wished Maxine would sit on down.

"It's on the back."

"I bought it because it was pretty. I don't care where it's made. Why don't you sit down and I'll cut up the weiners. I bet Paula's burning up in the car."

"She won't come in, Mother."

"Well why won't she?"

"You know why she won't--because she's crying. She feels that you broke a promise to her."

Dotsy saw that Maxine was ready to fly off the handle again. She wondered when Lucille was going to call back and she breathed heavily. "I didn't break anything to her," she finally said, "and you know it. Paula could have had that ring anytime she wanted if she'd asked for it."

"I'm asking for it for Paula," Maxine said. "I hope you don't make a liar out of me, too. I thought you cared more for her than you do."

Dotsy bit her lip and felt tears she couldn't hold back. She didn't try then, as Maxine pitched the dish on the sofa and hurried to the car. "Bless Pattie," Dotsy said, taking off her glasses, holding a handkerchief to her eyes to wipe the tears. She sat down, picked up the plate and threw it down the hallway and wished she hadn't when Stars jumped, afraid. "I'm not throwing it at you, honey," she said, and put her glasses back on. Then she stood at the screen and watched Maxine drive off. "Come on outside," Dotsy said, "at least you love me." She brought the Bible that sat on her side table. She left it on the plastic lawn chair and walked to the mailbox for the letter.

VIII. SUE

Dewey left the refrigerator door open while he decided what he wanted to eat. He frowned because he had a headache, sniffed the mingled odors of an opened package of bologna, cold asparagus in a shallow bowl, sliced cantaloupe, a partially unwrapped chocolate bar. He took the large jar of salad dressing off the swingout shelf, two moist slices of bologna, and the crescent of longhorn cheese. His head ached with a gentle rhythm across the back of his head. The refrigerator motor clicked on, but he spread the salad dressing onto the bread from the cabinet, added the meat slices, and cut the cheese into an even moon before he nudged the refrigerator door shut, then went to his room, lay on the twin bed next to the open window and ate the sandwich.

He thought about asking for the raise. If he didn't get it, he might get the furniture. He wished he'd said that he did prefer the blue lamps. Blue was his favorite color and the two lamps had chrome switches, and just at their bases, a white painted band. He wondered if he could ask for a coffee table. With the raise, he could pay down; without it, maybe his mother would give him one if he asked her. He chewed the spicy bologna and looked about his bedroom. He did not like the patterned carpet he had inherited from the living room, or the orange cast maple beds, the cluttered desk, or even the dull tan on the walls. The dark closet was filled with old clothes and at the bottom, shoes, cardboard boxes with toys and camping gear he had discarded. The green bedspread he lay on was thin and rumpled. He did not like the bedspread or the carpet or the open closet door that would not shut. He did not like what they reminded him of. And instead of the new sofa or the table and lamps, he wanted something entirely different. He thought Alice did, too. He did want to ask for a raise and he tasted bologna from his throat to the bottom of his stomach.

He turned toward the window when he heard the screen door next door slam. He heard Sue's "Yes," then watched her leave Jeannie's small white porch. He did not think that she could see him through the window screen. He noticed her slow as she walked onto his lawn. Usually Jeannie would walk with

61

her, and they would talk loudly close by his window; he knew they wanted him to come out.

He could swear Sue looked at him lying on the bed. He started to call out through the screen, to tell her to wait. Sue would probably use the sidewalk instead of walking by his window. He might not even see her again. He hurried out of bed, across the back porch, and out the backyard gate to the front. "Sue," he said, "wait up."

"You'd better wash your car," Sue said.

"I know." He felt better being outside, the sun hot and bright. He remembered that he had to get one of his mother's suitcases before he packed. She kept them in the top of the closet.

"What are you doing home?" she asked. "I thought you'd be busy."

"Nothing." Dewey said. "I have to go to the store later."

"You ought to wash your car," Sue repeated. "I'd be mad if I was Alice."

"I will."

"Jeannie and I started to go into your backyard to see the roses. We didn't know anyone was home for sure. She wanted to pick some."

"I was asleep," Dewey said. "No, I was thinking; I wasn't asleep. Let's go back and get off this hot pavement. Do you want some roses? You can have some. You can have all of them you want."

"Can I pick some of the yellow ones for Jeannie?"

"Come on," Dewey said. The back gate was so flush with roses that the flowers shook as he opened it for her. The climbing roses were every color. "You can have all of them you want."

"So you're out of school," Sue said, sitting at the picnic table.

Dewey sat across, facing her and the back of the house.

"You will be next year."

"If I get out! And I won't be getting married like Alice."

He wanted to tell her that she would be his choice if he hadn't picked Alice. He looked at her hand, her fingers longer than his because she was taller, bigger, but she wasn't fat. He didn't speak until he put his hand on hers. "You don't know," he said.

She let him squeeze her hand. "I shouldn't talk to you," she said.

"I haven't lied to you." He held her hand in both of his, then wrapped his fingers over hers. He wondered if Jeannie had seen them go into his backyard. If she could see over the fence from her back porch.

"I wish you would have," Sue said. "You never gave me a chance."

"You know how I feel about you." Dewey squeezed her hand again. "I never lied about that. I meant it."

"Uh huh."

"I did."

She looked at a shock of orange roses on the back fence. Dewey wanted, as he glanced at them too, to make her happy. He thought that he could put his finger on exactly what she wanted: thoughtfulness. That's why she liked him, and if he could have, he would have thought of only her as he did Alice but Alice didn't him, and he and Sue--but it was out of the question. No matter how much he thought of Sue, it would always be him and Alice.

Her hair was cut short. She had a puffy face, round, with brown eyes and a dimple in her left cheek. Once, when he had argued with Alice, and he and Sue were parked in front of her house, he had kissed her, his arms tight around her, then kissed her again and again, and this one time, because of the streetlight, he saw, up so close, how many blonde movie stars she resembled, how beautiful she was; he had inched up, his leg under him, and he looked at her and looked at her, remembering what she looked like when he was kissing and too close to see her face. "You're beautiful," he had told her, kissing her hair, his tongue along the rim of her ear, onto her cheek, her eyelids, his lips against hers. They had parked until they saw her mother peek out the front door.

"There's nothing to talk about," Sue said. "I'm happy for Alice."

"That doesn't mean we aren't friends. Do you mean that you don't want to know me simply because we aren't getting married? If you like me, you'll like me anyway. I haven't changed."

"I didn't say I didn't like you." Sue avoided his gaze.

"I can be close to you whether or not I'm with you." Dewey leaned across to the flowerbed and picked a rose.

"Smell it," he said. "If we want to we can have this flower. It can be ours and no one else's and it doesn't matter whether or not anyone knows because it's ours. Throwing it away would only be throwing away what we have--it wouldn't change that it's ours." He laid it on the table and Sue picked it up and sniffed it.

Dewey no longer cared if he had to ask for a raise. He didn't have to then, and he watched Sue smile and he thought that she could be a secret that he would always keep for himself. He wanted to tell her more than he had ever said before. He hadn't lied when he'd told her that she was beautiful or when he said that she was second. Not, 'I love you,' but he did; and he startled himself thinking that he had every intention to make love to her that afternoon. Her nose was very white against the rose. And her lips almost puffy, no lipstick.

"Doesn't it smell good?" he asked.

"Who planted them?" she asked.

"They were here when we moved in."

"I wish we had some. Have you ever been in our backyard? My brothers! You're lucky you don't have brothers!"

Dewey put his hand over hers again. "It doesn't make any difference to us," he said, "tell me you're not mad." He could feel her hand relax. He wanted to kiss it. He felt that she had something magnetic, her expression, the contour of her features, her size.

"I'm not mad at you!"

"And that you want to be friends."

She nodded.

"Then we will be," he said. "And it will belong to us just like the rose does." He felt her squeeze his hand too, and he looked at her dress, pushed way out because she was big-busted.

He opened cokes for them inside the kitchen. "I've never been inside your house," Sue said.

Dewey filled two glasses and sipped his. He listened for any sounds from the front door, or possibly a car in the drive. "Just a minute," he said, "okay?" He hurried into the dark living room--the orange curtains were drawn--and pushed in the button front door lock. "Sue," he said, to hide the click.

"I'm here." She leaned against the kitchen counter in the bright kitchen light. "You've got a dishwasher," she called.

"Yep. Want to come into the living room?"

"I'll stay here."

"Come here," he said, walking into the kitchen. "Give me a kiss to show we're still friends." She was two inches taller than he was; he leaned up, kissed her while she waited. She was quiet. She looked down; then she put her arm to his shoulder and pressed. Dewey brushed his tongue across her lips.

"There," she said. "Don't tell Alice I did that."

"It's between us. Everything is." He stood with his arm around her waist, his fingers flat across the buttons of her dress. His fingers were tingling. "Sue," he said. He thought when he looked at her that he was indeed getting married, that Alice was getting ready, and he put his arm around Sue, slowly, looking at her an inch from her face, then bringing his lips closer, his breathing heavy, his heart racing. He kissed her again, his palms across the snaps of her brassiere.

"Okay," she said. "I've got to go." But she left her arms at his waist.

He looked along the narrow hallway that led to his bedroom. The bare walls, dim, dingy, with a telephone stand at the end of the hall, the black phone with its receiver turned wrong, the coil hanging over the dial. A mirror above."Let me show you my room," he said. "You can trust me. No girl's ever been in my room."

"I've seen it," she said. "I can see inside through the screen."

"Come on," he said and tugged her arm.

He hadn't picked up his clothes from the day before. The unmade bed he'd lain on, made the room look worse. He went to the window and drew the blinds shut.

"I've got one of these," she said, holding a souvenir spike he had gotten in Nevada. "My uncle brought it to me." She sat on the bed and looked at the books he had in the bookcase headboards.

"There's nothing there." He never read those books. He didn't know where he'd gotten them, but many were Sunday School books. "I don't read much. You don't want to look at those." Despite himself, he felt impatient. He realized how ugly his room was.

"You've got annuals!" Sue said.

"You've seen those."

"Let's look at them. Please." She sat on the bed, an annual on her lap. The annual she chose had her picture in the center-fold. He glanced at her picture, too.

He put his arm around her as she turned the pages. He smoothed his hand across her back. There was the slightest fleshiness just about her waist; he rubbed teasingly, then hugged her while she squealed, held the annual high and told him to stop.

"Come on," he said, "put down the annual."

"No, I'm looking."

He lay on the bed. He liked having her in his room. He should have asked her long before, every week he could have arranged it, just the two of them. He imagined what she looked like without her blouse. He wanted to feel under her blouse. "Come here, kiss me."

Sue didn't shut the annual but she turned her lips toward him. "Come down here," he said, lying down.

She lay beside him. This is how it should be, he thought, you and me here. I don't care what happens, I'm glad. "Kiss me."

She didn't pooch her lips when she kissed. She left them still and she was so relaxed he wondered if she would protest at all what he had in mind. He lay on top of her, her head resting on his arms; he kissed, thinking that all he had to do was begin to unbutton her blouse. He readjusted; they were side to side. He unbuttoned the top button and she said nothing. He felt her holding her breath. He hesitated, listening to a sound he heard from the living room.

"What is it?" she asked.

"Nothing. Everyone's at work. It's just the house."

She relaxed, heavy against him. She's not going to stop me, Dewey thought. She's as excited as I am because she's so quiet. His fingers trembled. He wondered what she was thinking about his wedding day, why she didn't have more objections than he did. I feel great, he thought, smelling Sue's hair, fluffy, just shampooed. Then his hand was warm against her skin and he breathed heavier. When he next thought, it was 'I can't believe we're doing this,' and he didn't care what day it was. He could not believe that he had waited so long.

"Sue," he whispered, and she was paler, her eyes shut, her arms soft and at her sides. Then as he touched her, he was perfectly at ease, ready for more, almost ready to tease her, until she whispered, "Please hurry. Hurry."

They were still in bed when the telephone rang. Dewey answered it, and she covered up to her chin. He stood naked in the hallway, embarrassed at himself, chubby, now soft in the long mirror, his belly curved. "Hello."

"Aren't you coming back to the store? I've been waiting for you."

"Yes."

"What are you doing home? If I'd known you were home I would have had you bring me a sandwich for lunch. Are you coming down now?"

He noticed that she didn't mention the furniture. "Is Al there?"

"Yes, but he has to go to the bank later. Why don't you come on down now. And bring me some of that banana pudding in the refrigerator."

"I'm taking a bath," Dewey said. "I'll come later." Dewey waited for his mother's 'bye' then hung up. He saw that Sue had dressed while he was talking and she sat on his bed, and faced the blue curtain. He felt ridiculous with no clothes on, and slipped into his jeans and shirt, then sat beside her on the bed, barefooted.

"Come here," he said and lay back with her, feeling vaguely disappointed.

"Was that your mother?" she asked.

"Yeah."

"I thought it was because you sounded so nervous."

"Did I sound nervous?" He wondered if his mother could tell. "I guess I did. I am. Aren't you?"

"Yes."

"I haven't bought you a wedding present," Sue said. "I wasn't going to because I was mad at Alice."

"You don't have to buy me a present."

"I want to buy something special," she said. She leaned against the wall, and looked again at the books in the bookcase.

"Not what everyone else will buy you."

Dewey sat up too, glad that no one could catch them any longer. "There's no need," he said, wishing she'd quit looking at the books he never read.

"What would you like?"

"I think of us as separate," Dewey said. "I don't want a wedding present. I won't forget this afternoon."

"I won't either," she said. "You will."

"No, I won't. I'll never forget." He put his arm around her waist again, noticed her bulky skirt, her nylon blouse, her yellow hair at the nape of her neck.

"I wish you would call me sometime. I know we can't see each other, but we could talk. I thought you were being asinine."

"I wasn't. And we can see each other. Nothing will happen; you know that."

"We won't see each other," Sue said.

He could tell by her blush, and her head, almost ducked, her eyes not quite to his, that she wanted him to kiss her.

"I'll see you," he said, "whether you see me or not." He kissed, and thought that Alice kissed better, but less exciting to him. "Come on," he said, "kiss me back." She pressed hard with her flat lips until he could feel every tooth of hers against his mouth. "That's better."

"I'll see you," he said again, because he could not imagine giving her up, and he wished that it was not almost two-thirty and he could spend the afternoon with her in his house. He wanted to show her the cufflinks she had given him for the past two birthdays. He thought that he could tell her things because she wanted to listen to him. He wanted to undress her again. Yet he knew that she had to go and he had begun to hate it and think that regardless he could call her and they would talk.

At the screen he told her bye and watched her walk along the sidewalk to the street. She didn't glance back; just as if she'd left Jeannie's, she sauntered, the sunlight on her hair, her holding her shoes by the heel straps. Dewey thought, "I do love you in a way." He wanted to go after her. She was halfway down the block before she looked back, and he knew that she could not see him.

"I'll always think of you," he told himself, and went to straighten his bedroom. He smoothed the bedspread, then lay on it and thought, "It was here, right here," and he wished she hadn't left.

Then he heard the phone and went out the front door to his car. The steering wheel on his car was hot, and he put on the sunglasses he kept on the dash. He didn't mind asking for a raise, and he decided to ask for a coffee table, too. His mother had sounded in a good mood. He started the ignition and drove slowly, aware of the fine layer of dust on the carseats.

Sue had already gotten home. He noticed the blue trim on her white painted house as he passed by. What if she's pregnant? he thought. What can I do if she's pregnant? Dewey thought back very carefully to the moment and he tried to decide if she had gotten pregnant. She hadn't made any sounds, except that he knew that it hurt her because she had asked him to hurry. It didn't seem to him that she was pregnant, but he couldn't tell. He wished he had asked her how she felt. She should know, if he didn't. Maybe I should call her, he thought. No, I can't call. If she is, no matter how much I love Alice, I'll have to think of the baby. He gripped the steering wheel. Everybody does it--and sometimes they get caught, too. He could hear Lucille hypocritically say that she wouldn't have expected it of him, or Dotsy say, "There's an all-seeing eye watching you"--and Alice--so he wasn't safe just because the door was shut and locked and no one had caught them. That wasn't even the dangerous part. Don't be pregnant, he said, and he shivered, wondering what he would do if Alice too got pregnant that very night. You fool, he thought, remembering the package hidden in his bottom bureau drawer. He had bought the rubbers at a machine in a filling station over a year ago and put them away. So all the time he could have prevented it, with the rubbers that had excited and embarrassed him when he bought them, afraid that someone would notice them in his pocket before he got home and hid them, or that someone would know because of the expression of his lips. He could have explained using them to Sue, then he wouldn't have to worry. At school Stampoli had once said his girlfriend used to spew a hot coke up her if he didn't use a rubber. I can't ask Sue to do that, Dewey thought. I'll use the rubbers tonight and I'll tell Alice that I don't want a kid yet. I'll call Sue tomorrow and hang up if anyone else answers. If she's pregnant I'll tell her father myself. Stupid, he thought, feeling safe because the flimsy lock was pushed in. I wish someone had come home. I wish I knew if she was pregnant. He tried to think back again to decide.

IX. THE RAISE

"Yes, that's nice of him," Lucille said impatiently. She held the receiver between her neck and shoulder and stood, busy cleaning off her desk.

"Why I sure didn't expect it. I didn't even know who the letter was from because he mailed it in Miami. He paper clipped the fifty-dollar bill on top. I believe that's the most money anyone has ever sent me in the mail. He makes good money."

"Um hmmm."

"He always could when he wanted to. You should see his house now, Lucille. It's a mansion--no one could want better. He's got carpet a foot thick on his floors."

Lucille sat in the office chair that gave a poof when she sat down. "That's nice," she said.

"I'm going to write him this afternoon. I worry when he waits so long to write. He never did write like you girls did. I'll save his letter for you. Bless his heart. I wish he was here. Do you know how long it's been since I saw him? Two years!"

"You flew out there last summer, Mother."

"For three days. I don't call that a visit. He was here two years ago Christmas in that new Buick he'd bought Ann."

"I'm going to put this fifty dollars in the bank. I've got four twenties you've given me this month and I'm going to start paying out Perpetual Care for my cemetery lots with them. It doesn't cost but two hundred dollars in Seymour."

"I've got to go," Lucille said.

"Well, just a minute. I want you to tell Maxine something for me. I've gotten tired of bending over backwards to please her. If she's not speaking to me, I'm not speaking to her. I was sitting here thinking what my mother would have done if I'd talked to her like that."

"Uh huh." Lucille brushed her hair with one hand and held the receiver with the other. She brushed in quick strokes that made her short curls smooth out then pop back.

"Grown or not, she wouldn't have let a daughter sass her. And you can tell Maxine that I'm not having a thing to do with her until she apologizes.

"She's not going to apologize, Mother. She's mad at you."

"I don't care who she's mad at. I'm not speaking to her until she apologizes for calling me a liar. I didn't think when I gave Dewey the ring or I'd have known the other grandkids would feel bad. But you were here when I said I'd give Mama's ring to the first grandchild that married, weren't you?"

"No," Lucille said.

"I said I would. I thought Paula would be first, but I'll stick to my word. I don't want anyone calling me a liar without making themselves one. I guess I wasn't thinking how the other grandkids would feel. There's not just Paula, there's Sharon."

"There are the other boys, too."

"I guess I just wasn't thinking, but I'm not an Indian giver and I'm not going to ask Dewey for the ring, no matter who gets their feelings hurt. I guess I made an honest mistake like everybody does."

"I don't know," Lucille said.

"If it doesn't mean anything to him then I think Paula ought to have it. If he really wants it for Alice, then I want her have it."

"I don't think he has the money for another ring," Lucille said.

"He sure is young to get married, too. I kind of hate to see him do it."

"I do, too," Lucille said. "I hate to see him do it. I don't think he's mature enough." She said bye when Dotsy did, and she thought that she had a lot of work to do and nobody else was going to do it for her.

Dewey dreaded asking. He walked into the store, wished the bells attached at the top would not jingle so loudly, nodded to Tom, then went through the back door of the office. Bobbie, the secretary, was busy at the payment counter while Lucille added up invoices. He looked through the glass window but didn't see Al in his private office.

"Did you bring me anything to eat?" Lucille asked. "I'm starving."

"I thought you'd eaten." Dewey said.

"Oh you know I hadn't." Lucille opened her straw purse and took out her thick billfold. "Get us some pie at Hank's."

"I want some too," Bobbie said, "just a second," and she finished writing the payment.

"Have you ever tried Hank's pie?" Lucille asked the customer. "It's delicious."

"No, I haven't."

"He makes the best pie in town."

"Where's Al?" Dewey asked softly.

"I told you he wouldn't be here until this afternoon. You're early."

"You said he was here."

"He was, but he left. Have you decided to ask him for a raise?"

Dewey glanced at Bobbie, then nodded.

"Well tell him you're willing to work Sundays extra if we need you to."

"I don't want to work Sundays. We're not even open on Sundays."

"Tell him anyway," Lucille whispered, her eyebrows pinched together. "What kind of pie do you want, Bobbie? I'll get it--you can pay me later."

"I think I'll get custard."

"I don't know if I want chocolate or custard. The chocolate is delicious."

"I'll get a surprise," Dewey said. "I'll bring lemon."

"Oh, I don't want lemon!" Lucille chuckled. "Don't you bring lemon. Bring chocolate for me and if not chocolate, custard. Here." She put two dollars in his hand.

"I'm not going to work on Sundays," he said again.

Lucille made a quick face. She drew in her lips, flared her nostrils, and pinched her eyes together, and tried to make her eyes as hard as she could.

His eyes caught hers a second, then he turned furiously around.

"What kind are you going to get?" Lucille asked him.

He squeezed the money, then stuck it into his pocket. "I don't know."

"Do you want a barbeque sandwich?"

"No."

"His barbeque sure is greasy. Don't you think so, Bobbie?"

"The chipped is."

"I like his barbecued bologna though. Wait a minute, Dewey," she said in a complete change of voice. "Look in the window of Mercer's Jewelers when you pass."

Dewey nodded. He knew better than to ask why. He felt embarrassed about getting angry. Especially if Lucille had bought something for him and Alice at Mercer's. He hadn't expected another present. "I'll be back in a minute," he said. As he walked off, he stuck his hand in his pocket and was glad Al hadn't been at the store. Mercer's Jewelry was small and far from fancy; from the picture showcase window he could always see inside where Mr. Mercer sat, repairing watches, his thick glasses close up to the watch backs. Dewey usually stopped when he walked to Hank's and looked at the display of small jeweled rings, brassy gold watches, and china dusty from not having been wiped.

Their store was one of the last of the solid row of downtown stores; past the cleaners, frame houses with screened-in porches and weedy yards interspersed new brick buildings. Mercer's Jewelry was only a half a block away, next to a washateria. Dewey stared at the display and tried to decide which gift was his. He was curious but not disappointed that the window hadn't been rearranged and nothing had been taken out. He doubted Lucille was going to give him a new watch unless she possibly would give both of them one. China was more obvious, but easily more than Lucille would spend. She had probably decided on a single item, either the silver bowl or the blue and white crockery creamer and pitcher. When he peered up close, he saw the slightest black colored mars on the thin silver bowl; he thought that the crockery looked just washed, even wet around the blue rim.

Small stone diamond rings lined the back of the faded velvet shelf. Dewey glanced at them, patted the ring in his blue-jean pocket, and looked just at the door, at strings of pearls.

He wished he could buy his mother pearls—his mother and Alice. He spotted a double strand he would buy his mother if he could. And a smaller, more delicate string for Alice.

"Hello," Mr. Mercer said, wiping machine oil on the white apron tied about his waist. "Are you looking for something in particular, Dewey?" He had left the light on over a watch he fixed.

"No," Dewey said.

"Just looking?"

"Yes."

"Glad to have your business." Mr. Mercer returned to the workstool and put on the special glasses that gave off colored beams when he bent over the watch under the intense light.

He's not giving anything away, Dewey thought, thinking that perhaps his mother hadn't bought the crockery. Maybe she hadn't bought anything at all and was waiting to buy after hearing what he liked best. He decided not; she had chosen something. Mr. Mercer wasn't telling. Dewey remembered pie, looked at the different times all the watches and clocks in the window said, many of them running yet marking the wrong hours. Dewey hurried to the end of the block to Hank's.

He thought guiltily of Sue. When I call her, he thought, it'll be to say hello. She's not pregnant. There's nothing wrong with her this one time. Please God. He wished it again. Nothing at all wrong, he thought. If Sue had told, he would already have heard from her parents. He decided as he went into Hank's that he would get a chipped beef with pickle relish, mustard, onions, and one of the sweet green peppers that Hank bought in Mexico.

"Aren't you getting married?" Hank asked, his tee shirt drenched, his fat shoulder's pink through the material.

"Chipped?"

"Yes."

"It's free. My present, Dewey." Hank dropped an extra amount on the fluffy bun.

"Thanks." Dewey tried to avoid the high meringue pies on top of the counter.

"There." Hank handed Dewey the thinly wrapped sandwich. "What do you want to drink?"

"Just water."

"It's free today. Want a coke? Pie?"

"Nope." Let me pay, Dewey thought. I can't ask for three pieces of pie. He noticed a whole custard pie covered with wax paper. "Let me pay for the sandwich," he said.

"Not a chance. You'll pay for getting married the rest of your life. Everything's free today."

"It's good. Thanks."

"Here's a Nehi, Dewey. I know you like oranges."

He preferred them with barbecue sandwiches. He took the cold bottle and sat in one of the blonde wooden chairs. "Thanks," he said again. Then Hank answered the phone and Dewey wished he hadn't ordered the sandwich. He didn't want to upset Lucille by not buying pie. He ate slowly, and hoped that Hank would go out back and one of his daughters would wait on customers.

The barbeque had a fiery taste that the strong orange quenched.

"You're a good boy," Hank said. "I'm glad that you're getting married."

"I am too."

He wondered if Alice would like the blue crockery too and he counted to himself: a new sofa, two end tables and two lamps even if they were green, the blue crockery or something else, unexpected, from the jewelry store, and he admitted to himself, a raise to boot. He imagined how excited Alice would be, and he was too, adding it up. Asking for a raise seemed little compared to what all he could get. He mulled while finishing the sandwich, imagined that Lucille had gotten them a whole set of china too, and while he was at it, the silver bowl with the marks that would probably come off with silver polish, and a coffee table and the blue lamps. He could imagine a new blue chevy with air-conditioning and radio, and a vacuum cleaner for Alice--their pick of *anything* they wanted at the store, and all the money in the world so he could buy presents and have everything he wanted. He grinned, thinking how the furniture and crockery and raise had shrunk.

"Thanks for the barbecue," he said. "It's good."

"Bring in your wife." Hank sliced an oblong brisket with a dull-colored, sharp knife.

"I will."

Outside, Dewey rubbed his stomach and wished he hadn't eaten all the sandwich. A fold of his belly pooched over his tight belt. He walked the opposite direction of the store and ducked into the Skillet that smelled of onions. He didn't know the girl behind the counter. He sat on a red-covered stool and scrutinized the pie in the glass pie case. He didn't like their tough pie crust.

"Have you got any custard?" he asked.

"No. Do you want something to drink?"

"No, thanks. I'll take three pieces of apple pie to go."

While she wrapped the small slices, he dropped a dime into the small jukebox selector and punched the buttons for "Blue Suede Shoes" and "Tennessee Waltz." He listened to the fast notes, tapped his foot, and watched people downtown stroll past.

Walking back, he hummed to himself and looked down Main Street as if it were his. He balanced the paper plate on his palm. He thought he'd ask Al quick, have the raise, then call Alice.

"Where did you get this awful pie?" Lucille asked. "It tastes like cardboard."

"It sure does." Bobbie wrapped the napkin around hers after the first bite. "Do you want mine?"

"It's not bad," Dewey said. "Hank was out so I went to the Skillet." The pie tasted mildewed to him.

"If I weren't hungry, I wouldn't eat another bite," Lucille said. "What kind is it supposed to be?" She gobbled down the rest of hers. "Thank goodness. Get us a coke to take away the taste." She laughed, while Dewey got three nickels from the tin change box for cokes and bought them all one.

"Here," he told Bobbie and handed her one of the half frozen cokes. Dewey left the machine as cold as possible because he liked the cokes icy. Lucille took a big gulp that burned her throat. "Oh that's strong!" she said.

"I like the pie," Dewey said, taking another sweet bite that quickly turned sour on his tongue. "It's apple."

"Why it tastes awful!" Lucille laughed and drank more coke. She brushed the crumbs from her skirt. "Did you go by Hank's?"

He knew she meant Mercer's Jewelry, not Hank's. He nodded, waiting.

"You've got barbecue sauce on your cheek," she said. "Why didn't you bring me a sandwich?"

"Do you want one?"

"Not after that pie. Do you, Bobbie?"

"No thanks. I don't think I'll even eat supper."

"Did you look in Mercer's window?" Lucille asked. "I like his jewelry store better than any in town."

"Yes."

"Don't you like it, Bobbie?"

"I sure do. I take my watch to him whenever anything goes wrong with it."

"Did you see anything you liked, Dewey?"

"Yeah." He drummed his fingers on his knee while he sat.

"Did you see a ring you like?"

"A ring?"

"He's got pretty diamond rings in his window. I bet Alice would like to have one."

"I've got a ring." Dewey wondered what she meant. He rubbed a thumb over his pocket to make sure the ring was still there.

"I bet Alice would rather have a diamond. I would."

Dewey glanced at his mother's chip diamond ring in a silver mounting. "I'd rather have a band."

"You're supposed to, you're a man."

"I don't like diamond rings," he said. "I can't afford one if I did."

"You don't have to get a big one. I bet Alice would rather have one. Don't you, Bobbie?"

"I would," Bobbie said. "I'll never forget when Joe gave me mine."

"Did Dotsy say something about the band? She gave it to me this morning."

"Have you got it?"

"At home. But Alice doesn't want a diamond ring. I don't either."

"Ask her," Lucille said.

"Why should I ask her?"

"Because it's her ring. Dotsy said that she bet Alice didn't even want it and she should have given it to Paula."

"She didn't say that."

"You don't have to believe me." Lucille turned around to the desk, her lips tight, her eyes narrow. Bobbie quietly began to post payments into the Open Account books.

"Why would she say that?" Dewey said. "She gave me the ring. She didn't have to."

"You ask Alice," Lucille said. "If she wants a diamond she should get one. It's her wedding."

Dewey could see that Al was in his office and talked to a salesman. He thought of the raise. "Al's back," he said.

Lucille said nothing. She rubbed fingers on an invoice to check the bill.

"How much should I ask for?" he said.

"It's your raise," Lucille pushed back her chair and walked to the small gift wrap corner at the rear of the office. She glanced back.

Dewey could smell her perfume and watched as she switched from the slip-on shoes she wore in the office to the black uncomfortable ones she wore from home. She pitched her soft shoes under the counter. He followed her.

"You ask Alice," she said lowly. "It won't hurt you."

He nodded.

"Will you?" she asked.

"Yes. Where are you going?"

"Al will give you the raise. I'm going to Soroptomist; I'm already late." She made a clomp with her high-heeled shoes. "Is my skirt straight?"

"Yes," Dewey said, and he glanced again toward Al busy in his office as Lucille hurried out, the door chimes jingling. "It's just me," she called to the salesmen as she left.

Dewey stood outside the office without watching the two men inside. He sat alone on the low bench kept for children waiting while their parents shopped. The colorful numbers and blocks the kids had played with were scattered on the floor. Dewey crossed his legs, uncrossed them, bent over and retied his brown shoelaces, then sat straight on the foam-covered bench. He avoided looking through the glass directly in front of him. He stacked the blocks in a neat row away from the aisle.

He thought his mother must have already gotten Al to agree to the raise. The money seemed smaller the more he thought about it, and he looked across at the gift corner and tried to spot an ashtray he might buy that would be pretty with the coffee table. He was sure that all he had to do was ask. He stuck his thumb in the waist of his bluejeans and felt his pulse beating in his stomach. He could feel the knocking under his shirt, too; he glanced into the office, but Al still listened to the salesman holding swatches for sofas.

Lucille usually did ask Al first, then told Dewey to ask. In the summers when Dewey worked at the store, Lucille took her time dressing and told Dewey to ride with Al. Dewey had ridden beside Al a hundred times during the short trip to town; he saw each house, its yard, its windows, the sloping roofs, saw the chugholes in the road, anyone along the street, dogs in the yards, then the white filling stations, the tire dealer's, and with relief, the corner where they turned to the store. One house close to where they lived had a nursery with firs and neatly kept potted shrubs, and a greenhouse out back. Beside this house were several vacant lots. Dewey, bored, had often started a conversation such as "I wonder how that nursery stays in business," or "These lots would make a good park," or "That white house is where Joyce Malone lives. She's really good in my algebra class." Al would nod, even grin sometimes, or say, "Uh hmm," but nothing more; Dewey would pause, trying to think what he could say next, and wishing all the while that his mother hadn't pushed them together. Once he asked, "What are you going to do today?" and Al grinned, shook his head and said incredulously, "I'm going to work." Dewey nodded, embarrassed even that he was nodding, thought harder, and asked, "Are you going to do anything special?" Al had stopped at a light though; the pliers on the dashboard of the pick-up fell to the floor and Dewey bent to pick them up, his nose full of dust. He was grateful, looking at the webbed seat covers and the cab floor littered with gum wrappers, screw drivers, wadded delivery tickets, cash register slips, chunks of wood, and a greasy rag. Thank God I'm down here, he thought, then opened and closed the pliers the rest of the trip and didn't care if Al hadn't answered him.

"Oh you two ride together, I'm late!" Lucille would say, and Dewey would walk to the pick-up, get in, wait for Al who, without a word, or a look in his direction, started the pick-up and backed slowly out the drive. Al kept his hat on while he drove: occasionally he lighted a cigar and if it went out, chewed on it.

Dewey glanced through the office window and caught, for a second, Al's eye. Both of them glanced away. Dewey wondered again if he should ask for a raise; he looked at a maple lamp on an end table, a lamp with a chintz shade and a crystal top and he thought how ugly the lamp was and how uneasy he felt, just in that past second.

He didn't think it often but as he waited and looked through the office window, he wished he had a real father. One he could talk to, who would frankly tell him whether or not he asked, if he could have a raise. "I don't even want a raise," he thought, wondering why his mother went to the trouble of making him ask, and of telling Al herself. He wished really, that he had someone on his side, a father, who wanted him to have a raise. His father lived two hundred miles away but Dewey never saw him.

He wished his father was sitting behind that desk, but a different father from the one two hundred miles away. He wanted one who knew something about how he felt and wanted him to feel even happier because he was happy that he was getting married. He saw Al now as he saw a stranger, a man he didn't know and who not only didn't know him but who wanted to turn his face away, to say nothing.

Then Dewey knew it was lost: there would be no raise. The furniture did not matter and he sat, humble pie on his face, his eyes empty.

When the salesman had left, Al sat at the desk and did not look out the window to motion Dewey in.

"Are you busy?" Dewey asked at the door.

Al shook his head. He waited to hear what Dewey had to say.

"Mother's gone to Soroptomist hasn't she?" Dewey asked.

"No. She's in the office."

"No, she's already gone." Dewey looked furiously about the office for something to focus on. "I wanted to ask you about something." He could plainly see that Lucille hadn't mentioned it to Al. "Since I'm getting married, I'd like a raise," he said. He wanted it then, as he said it, and he thought he'd earned it and he knew how happy Alice would be. Please, he thought, let's don't fuss about it.

Al sat straight in the swivel chair and the springs creaked. He patted the back of his hair with his palm.

"I'll work Sundays if I have to," Dewey said.

"How long have you been working?" Al asked.

Dewey thought of the summers he had spent at the store-- all but one--when he had worked at the drug store down the block. "Since I graduated," he said.

Al chuckled. "That was a month ago."

Dewey couldn't ask if his work had been okay. He wanted the raise and he determined that he was going to have it. The raise was like something Al held a thousand of and wouldn't give a single one because he didn't want to.

"Can I have it?" Dewey said, his voice high, obviously angry.

"Are you working today?" Al picked his unlighted cigar from the ashtray and chewed on the end.

"I'm getting married today."

"No, you can't have a raise," he said.

Dewey slammed the office door and wished the glass would break. He hurried past the office, ignored Bobbie who looked up at him. He got into his car and he started the engine and felt that he had known it all along. There was no raise, no present at Mercer's nothing. He drove toward Oak and turned the radio up high.

Dewey stopped at the telephone booth in the half block parking lot of the First Baptist Church. He stuck his keys in his pocket then fingered up a nickel. His fingers trembled; he wanted to make a fist and hit Al in the face. He dropped the nickel in the coin slot. I shouldn't have slammed the door, he thought. I should have kept my temper. He listened to the dial tone and wondered if after all he should call Alice. He didn't have the sofa and the tables. He sure didn't have a raise. Nobody had to tell him whose side his mother would be on. He hesitated and read some of the scratches on the phone booth. When the church had bought the filling station, they had torn down the building and pumps and paved the adjoining vacant lot, but had left the telephone booth on the corner. He had never used it before. I don't care what he tells, Dewey thought. It made his knees weak to think how Al whispered on him and Lucille then corrected or griped, and pretended that she knew on her own and no one had told her. But this time seemed different, more important and he couldn't say why. He wasn't just angry at Al and his mother; he didn't want the blue china at Mercer's Jewelry or the lamps for the tables. He hated the small booth without a stool to sit on and the towering square red brick church without a steeple. He felt quite sensibly that he wanted something that he had never had and didn't know what, but the desire rose in his chest and caused him to look miserably at the telephone, his teeth clicking against each other.

He dialed the numbers deliberately, swallowed, and hoped that Alice would answer.

"Hello?" she said, her voice not at all understanding or thoughtful, as if she didn't expect to hear from him.

"Alice?"

"Dewey?"

She sounded genuinely surprised. Who did you expect? he thought. Why didn't you know I'd call; we're about to be married. He said nothing and waited, irked at how long she waited, too. He couldn't believe she didn't want to talk.

"Where are you?"

He felt embarrassed on the corner in the parking lot. "I'm downtown," he said.

"What's wrong? You sound funny."

The anxiety made him feel better, more in control of himself. He silently admired a new yellow Ford that turned the corner. That's what I wish I had, he thought.

"Dewey?"

"Nothing," he said. He knew that Al would tell. The secretary had looked up when he slammed the door and a customer had been at the payment desk. "I've lost my job," he said.

"You lost your job?"

"I lost my job."

"Why?" He could tell that Alice didn't believe him. She didn't think his parents would boot him out the door.

"Because I asked for a raise," he said quietly.

"What?"

"I asked for a raise," he said.

"I can still work at the draft board. You don't need a raise, Dewey."

"Yes I do," he said, thinking that Alice was as uncaring as any of them. All she wanted was for him to work. She didn't care. He wanted to yell into the telephone at her.

"Who fired you?"

"What does it matter."

"Well who did?"

"It doesn't matter. I don't have a job." He was furious she didn't understand.

"But we're getting married today."

"I don't know about that either," he shouted. Once he said it, he felt cold inside. He knew how unexpected it was for her, even if he didn't mean it. Like my getting fired, he thought, and quickly corrected himself, well like his telling me that I can't have a raise. He could feel his anger flowing thick and fast until he decided, when she said nothing, to hang up at once. He clicked down the receiver. He looked at his dirty yellow car. He wished none of it had happened and he panicked, feeling in his pocket. He felt the keys and change, and for a minute he couldn't feel the wedding ring.

X. ALICE WORRIES

Alice heard the click then the dial tone. "Dewey," she said. He's hung up, she thought. She felt her cheeks hot and she wanted to slam the receiver too. She smiled uneasily, her eyes on the list of numbers beside the phone book as her mother hurriedly passed, carrying freshly ironed blouses on wire hangers. Her mother didn't look or speak, but Alice said, "Yes, that will be all right, goodbye," and carefully replaced the receiver. She walked into her bedroom and felt as noticeable as if she'd been caught in a lie. She could hear her mother in the other bedroom and Alice sat on the squeaky springs and rubbed a pimple that hurt on her neck. She leaned back against one of the ruffled polka dot pillows and tried to look out the half-opened blinds. She waited for her mother to return to her ironing in the kitchen.

"There," Amy said and walked into Alice's bedroom. "We may as well finish your suit. I've got the ironing done." She sounded as impatient as Alice felt.

"Do you want to sew on it now?"

"I thought you wanted to take it with you."

"I do." She followed her mother into her brother's room where her mother kept the treadle machine pushed up against the wall. Amy already had the suit out and on the half bed. It was light green, with no button holes. Alice thought how nice a suit it was and hoped Dewey liked it. She had chosen the pattern for him.

Amy shut the door and Alice slipped off the skirt and blouse she wore. She expected the phone to ring again any minute. She wanted to stay in her bedroom close to the phone. She didn't understand why he hung up. She hooked the skirt, then slipped the top over her hair. The neck caught a loose bobby pin in her hair and pulled, causing her to make a face. She had a tender scalp.

Amy already had a mouthful of straight pins.

Alice listened for the telephone while Amy marked the hem with the pins. The suit top choked her and she thought the material puckered.

"Is this where you want it?" Amy held the material just below Alice's mid-calf.

"Yes, that's okay."

"I don't think it's too long. What shoes are you going to wear with it?"

"I don't know." She thought she heard the phone, then realized it was the radio. "Dewey's going to call back," she said.

"Stand straight."

Alice stiffened while Amy worked. I should have asked him what happened, she thought. I can't believe he got fired. She blushed when she looked at her mother.

"Does that seem right to you?" Amy talked with the pins in her mouth. She pinned a last marker and stuck the extra pins together, in a knot, into the pin cushion.

"Is it even?"

"It looks even. Let me get the measure."

Alice stood still but looked into the narrow full length mirror on the back of the door. It was plain as daylight that the neck was too tight and puckered.

"It's even," Amy said, measuring. She hung the yellow tape measure around her neck and stepped back to look. "It's real pretty."

"How about the neck?"

"It looks all right to me." Amy pressed her thumb against one of the puckers, trying to flatten the material. Alice could tell by Amy's face that the neck did pucker. "I followed the pattern exactly," Amy said. "Maybe it's the material. Does it feel tight?"

"It chokes at the neck."

"I guess it doesn't look right." Amy looked at the neck, then at Alice. "I'll have to take it apart. Take it off and I'll work on it now."

Alice planned to wear the suit on the honeymoon and she slipped it off, wishing Amy had been more careful. She thought that if she'd made a hundred dresses for someone, she'd be able to fit it exactly--even without them. She hoped Dewey liked it and she wondered what she would do if he didn't call back. She felt guilty that Amy had to take the suit apart and she pulled it off, lay it on the bed and looked at it. "Here," she said, "see where it puckers."

"Yes. I don't know if I can get that out."

"I've got to wash my hair." Dewey had hung up before, when they had argued over the phone, but he had called right back. She wished the phone would ring.

"Go ahead." Her mother pumped the treadle with her foot and the machine hummed as it stitched.

"Can I help?"

"No," Amy said. "I can do it."

Alice could hear the machine clearly even from her bedroom with the door shut. She got her lemon shampoo and a tube of acne medicine, her green housecoat that smelled like her sheets, and locked herself into the small bath. She had decided to clean up the closet and finish packing the boxes later. In fact she had covered most of her bed with mementoes she didn't want to store in boxes. Things that shouldn't be put away, but that she knew Dewey would think she was silly to keep: pictures of herself in California, a sand dollar from Galveston, her halves of theatre tickets, worn-out purses she hadn't rummaged through but she wanted to keep because they were stuffed with notes. She found a notebook of high school themes and old report cards.

She stood in the bathtub and shut the venetian blinds, then stepped out, turned on the hot water, undressed, and sat on the edge of the tub. She finally felt a sense of privacy. She leaned over, her elbows on her knees, her face on her palms. She felt another loose hairpin in her hair, took out the pin and laid it on the sink. Why doesn't he call? she wondered. He had been upset with his parents a hundred times before, but he'd never gotten mad at her about it. If we don't get married, she thought, and she realized that she couldn't stay home, not with her parents and her brother, the same dull bedroom, the mowed back lawn with a few flowers, mostly hollyhocks near the garage, the tiny living room her parents sat in every night.

She wouldn't stay whether Dewey married her or not.

She reached over and turned off the hot water; she could hear the sewing machine as if her mother stitched just outside the door. The bathroom was steamy; her legs were hot and sweat trinkled down her shoulders.

She felt like someone was pointing a finger at her and she didn't see why. Dewey was being unfair. He had hung up. "I only asked him what happened," she thought. "What if I hung up on him?"

Her palms were wet from the steamy room. Alice sniffed and turned off the hot water. She couldn't believe that Dewey would leave her because she would never leave him. She trembled as she thought: maybe he doesn't love me any more. She bent over, her skin reddish, her ribs jerking as she let herself cry.

She sniffed again. She opened the cabinet by the tub, took out a box of Tide and sprinkled some into the water. Tide was good for her oily skin; then thin suds on top fizzed and she waved her hands against the water to build more white suds. The Tide made her nose itch. She sat up in the tub and scrubbed her face with a pink washrag.

Maybe I should call him, she thought, and decided that she would if he hadn't called before she finished her hair.

She had never expected to marry him. When she was in the sixth grade, she knew exactly who she was going to marry. Janie had told her that she was the cutest girl in school, and Alice could tell that the others thought so, too. She wore long blonde curls that took Amy hours to fix, and Amy sewed the plaid, ruffled dresses everyone praised. Alice knew then that she would marry Carl--he was her first boyfriend.

Even now she remembered him as a perfect angel. He was the best-looking boy in class: blonde like her, his hair short, him taller than the other boys and polite. She knew what it was like then to have the boy any other girl would have given her eye teeth to have. Once, when Carl had taken her to the movie, she had held hands with him and watched the movie-- she couldn't remember what it was--and she had planned out their life together. He had been her ideal boyfriend, just for her. So much of her life had been dream, especially then, fantastic dreams impossible for her to even think of now: strange twists of fate that made her a princess in disguise, the same twist that brought her Carl only exaggerated, dreams

88

whereby she could honestly be a sincere Christian in Africa, and after her pimples came and she was no longer popular, dreams that made her identify with movie stars on the screen: flawless complexion, fluffy hair and bright eyes with the inevitable protagonist situation that she believed was hers. Maybe afterwards, in the glare outside--disappointed that it was after all still bright and only the middle of the afternoon while she had expected a continuous magic dark theatre outside for her--she felt a pang, but every movie she would forget again and she looked forward to movies, excited, entertained, positive that she would become that dream.

And now, in the bathtub, she wondered if the brassiere she had washed and hung on the mop handle in the hot water heater closet was dry, and she thought that really she didn't want to daydream. She wanted Dewey and poor as they were, she wanted their life together and nothing that she wouldn't understand or even like any more. She wanted him to call. She rubbed soap on her cheeks. She hoped that her face wasn't broken out more than usual and she promised that she would wash and roll her hair three times if necessary until it was perfect.

She soaped her thin shoulders with her palms, then sloshed water over them. The hot water made her shoulders red. Whatever I do, she thought, I won't stay here. She had outgrown the old bathroom and the small bright mirror on the medicine cabinet, the haunting cries of her brother and his friends playing outside, the sewing machine, even the silence when she turned down the knob to let the water drain--she remembered exactly when the drain had quit gurgling and the water quickly draining--now, she was past that, older, even if it had been her life. She wished Dewey would call. She wished she hadn't asked her mother to resew the suit and that her bed wasn't cluttered with things she wished she hadn't even taken out of the drawers. She didn't want to see Laura's invitation to the eighth grade party after graduation or the pictures of Carl or her report cards, all A's, neatly stacked and now two inches thick, wrapped around with a wide rubber band.

She scooted way down in the tub until her neck hurt and the tile felt hard against her legs. She wet her hair, reached for the yellow shampoo and her eyes squeezed tight, began to massage the lather through her short hair. Then she sat up, her hair white and soapy. She remembered her father's razor--it was open and the blade clean and dry, on top of the shelf above the commode. She needed it to shave her legs. She always changed blades first, and she didn't use his shaving soap, she used Ivory.

The shampoo streamed along her face, and she stroked her hands upwards, to keep the thick suds in her hair. Then she bent over, her back aching, turned on the water and rinsed her hair. The Tide made her bath water sudsy too, and she squeezed the water from her hair, then poured another handful of shampoo--she used a lot to make her hair light and soft--and thought of all she had to do: roll and dry her hair, fix her nails, shave her legs, pack the suitcases and clean up her room. She rinsed her hair again, ran her fingers along it to make sure that it was squeaking clean, then wrapped a towel around her wet hair and leaned back in the tubful of water. Her face was red with heat.

She believed that she could depend on Dewey. He was more punctual than she was; he did what he told her he would and he had never lied to her. She thought that she knew exactly how he felt about her--just as she felt about him. I can work at the draft board, she thought, it doesn't matter whether or not he's lost his job. I'll call him in a minute. I don't mind the draft board. Not if I'm married, too.

She never had thought that he'd stay at the store forever anyway. She didn't care if he ever ran the store. He cleaned up, helped deliver and worked part-time in the office. They didn't give him any responsibility. She thought he could do so much more. She thought Dewey had to go on to college even if she couldn't. Because of what he was going to be. She didn't know exactly why she hadn't thought of it before. She soaped her arms and ran the white bar across her neck and her small breasts. She rubbed in little circles. Why should he stay at the store? She couldn't think of a single reason, and that's what they had been going to do. They hadn't even discussed his quitting! She better understood why he was so upset when he called. He wanted to go to college as much as she did. She couldn't wait to tell him that it was good he was fired because now she would work at the draft board and he could go to school. She didn't care what he wanted to be. She thought he'd be a good lawyer. Or a scientist. That appealed to her more: a scientist, the difficult lab work that required ideas, the pungent smells she remembered from chemistry, the lab itself: a series of sinks, test tubes, bunsen burners, and Dewey in a white laboratory jacket and attempting to discover some important natural secret.

She stepped out of the tub, and hurriedly dried off with a thin pink towel that wilted. She hurried, slipped on her robe, then, in the hallway, felt embarrassed that she and Dewey had argued. She hadn't understood and she was guilty, too; anyway, the quarrel was finished because she had a perfect solution. She took the phone into her mother's bedroom. The short cord just wrapped around the corner and the door barely closed. Alice grinned, realizing that she was humming into the telephone.

"Sheppard's Furniture," Lucille answered.

"Is Dewey there?" Alice asked.

"Is this Alice?"

"Yes." She didn't want to talk to his mother. Lucille made her ill-at-ease, but she was always nice.

"He's not here," Lucille said. "When I got back from lunch he had already taken off."

"Oh."

"Have you talked with him?"

Alice couldn't lie. She didn't understand why Lucille talked as if Dewey should be at work. "Yes," she said.

"Well, where is that boy? He's not home."

Then Alice realized that of course Dewey wouldn't be at the store. She wondered why he wasn't home.

"I want you to talk to him," Lucille said. "Something's wrong with him."

"Nothing's wrong with him," Alice said.

Lucille whispered. "Yes there is. This afternoon he insulted Al. Did you know that? He didn't give Al time to answer when he asked for a raise; he just stormed out. Did he tell you that?"

Alice held the telephone close to her ear. The black receiver pressed against the thin towel wrapped around her wet hair. She didn't know what to believe. She didn't want to say anything either, but she thought 'you're lying,' and she was silent.

"We can't afford to give him a raise. I guess that's when he called you, and he was upset because Dotsy didn't want to give him the wedding ring. She thought you didn't want it."

"I wanted it," Alice said, surprised. She wondered if Dewey said she didn't. He hadn't even mentioned the ring.

"Well, she didn't think you did. She thought you wanted a diamond ring. I want you to talk to him," Lucille said. "He needs to apologize to Al." Lucille paused. "I'm embarrassed at the way Dewey acted. I hope you can talk to him."

"I don't believe that," Alice said firmly.

"You don't believe me?"

"No. I don't think Dewey would insult Al."

"You're impertinent," Lucille said. "I don't appreciate it." She hesitated, but Alice said nothing.

Alice heard the phone click as Lucille hung up the receiver. Alice felt scared to death. She hung up too, and she went back into the bathroom and sat on the chenille covered commode lid. She wondered where Dewey was. Dewey, she thought to herself as hard as she could, Dewey, I'm sorry. And she thought that suddenly she understood much of what he told her that had been troubling him all along. She had paid no attention to it. In fact, she hadn't really believed him. She trembled; both Dewey and his mother were angry with her.

Alice took the brush rollers from the box she kept them in. First she combed her wet hair smooth and straight, then she took a roller, pulled out the pink plastic stobs stuck in it from the last time she'd rolled it and pulled it off, stob and all--it never hurt because when her hair was warm the rollers loosened and came off gently. She began to roll up her hair.

She listened to the thump of the sewing machine and thought how hard Amy worked. She combed a wide strand of hair, fixed the end around the roller, and curled it tightly to her scalp. She listened for the phone. The thumping of the machine seemed louder. She thought of all the dresses Amy had made for her. She wished that she could tell Amy what had happened and she looked into the mirror, her eyes perfectly still. She rolled her hair.

I didn't know. The words seemed completely different to her. *I didn't know,* or I wouldn't have said what I did to Dewey. She glanced at the chrome edge that held the mirror and her reflection. Some of the mirror was worn black at the corners. I didn't want to make him unhappy. She could see that there was something dark she didn't understand but had been there. She was cut off from seeing it. Yet it had been in the light, under a bright bulb, just ahead of her. She looked at her pale eyelashes in the mirror. It was in no way fair that she had been expected to know. If he did not call, it was unforgivable and both of them would be wrong. I didn't know, she thought.

"Alice," Amy called.

Alice blew her nose, flushed the Kleenex and looked into the mirror. Her eyes were still red.

"Alice," Amy called again.

"I'm coming." She walked down the little hall and into the bedroom. The new jacket no longer puckered around the stitches. Her mother had neatly folded the tape measure and picked up loose threads, snipped off as she sewed, that always fell onto the hardwood floor.

"I think it turned out okay," Amy said.

Alice tried on the jacket. The neck fit perfectly. "It's beautiful," she said, holding out her arms and looking at the sleeves.

"I think it turned out real pretty."

"Thank you."

Amy raised the machine, lowered it into the cabinet, and cleaned off the flat covered top. She didn't speak.

"Did anyone call?" Alice asked.

"When?"

"While I washed my hair."

"You were closer to the telephone than I was. I can't hear it ring when I'm sewing."

That's true, Alice thought. "You didn't hear it ring, did you?"

"No. Who's supposed to call?"

She started to fib, but she didn't want to. She didn't think she should. She nervously checked the scarf she'd tied around her rollers. "I hoped Dewey would."

"Why he's not going to call again. He's probably as busy as you are."

Alice looked at her mother quietly and sat on the edge of her brother's bed. She thought that Amy might be able to tell her what she should do. She spoke lowly so Amy would know it was private. "He had an argument with his parents," she said.

Amy closed the bedroom door although they were alone in the house. She put back on her glasses she used when she sewed or read.

"Did he tell you that?" Amy asked.

"Yes."

"What did they argue about?"

"Dewey asked for a raise. He thinks he's lost his job."

"What did he do that for?" Amy asked. "He's only worked there since school was out."

"He's worked there summers since we were in the eighth grade."

"For his allowance. What's he going to do for another job?"

"I've got my job at the draft board."

"Are you going to work even after you're married?" Amy asked. She had never worked a day since she and Ed had married, except for one weekend she'd clerked in a department store, but she had decided that even weekends were too much and Ed had agreed.

"When you start out married life, you're poor. You can't expect to have everything given to you."

"I don't want it to be."

"You have to live where you don't want to, and you have to do without. When your daddy and I married, we were doing good to buy groceries and pay the rent. He made twenty dollars a week."

Alice listened because her mother seldom talked about how poor they had been. Alice thought they were poor now.

"We rented an apartment in Galveston. It was on the third floor and we used the bathroom on the second. We didn't want to live there--we had to. What else did Dewey say?"

Alice was too embarrassed to tell that Dewey had hung up on her. She wished she hadn't mentioned the quarrel.

"You'd better tell him to ask for his job back."

He's going to go to college, Alice said to herself. She couldn't say it aloud, but she realized that it was the right thing to do. She couldn't listen to Amy without blushing.

"He got fired," she said, feeling justified.

"Fired? He'd better ask for his job back if he wants to get married."

Alice folded the suit carefully and wished she hadn't asked her mother to sew it.

"I don't know what he got fired for," Amy said. "It's not my business and I'm going to stay out of it. You should, too. I just said that if Dewey is getting married he has to work."

"He didn't quit his job. He was fired."

"What are you going to live on?"

"I can still work at the draft board."

Amy nervously felt in the pockets of her housedress. "You couldn't even pay for all the clothes you wanted," she said. "You had to put them on layaway." She hesitated. "A man's not happy if he can't support his family, Alice. You know how your father wouldn't let me work. It hurts a man's pride."

"I can get my job back at the draft board."

"It's different when you get married," Amy said. "Dewey won't want you to work and you'll have more than you can do at home."

He's going to go to college, Alice thought.

Amy frowned, then took off her glasses. She waited, and neither she nor Alice spoke. "I'd better get your cake iced," she said. "Do you want to ice it?"

"I've got to finish packing."

Amy stepped out of the room and into the bright kitchen. Alice could see her, the shining linoleum floor clean under Amy's polished white houseshoes. Alice sat on her brother's bed and rubbed her hand across the patchwork quilt her grandmother had made. She noticed a triangular square of blue and white plaid material from her favorite skirt in the eighth grade. She wished she had the skirt. Then she thought that she didn't want the skirt--she had torn it one summer on their vacation to California. She couldn't help then, thinking how much she disliked Amy. She embarrassed herself thinking it and looked up, in case her mother was watching.

She could hear her light the gas oven. She felt ungrateful and she wondered if she was being un-Christian.

She knew exactly where her mother was in the kitchen because the pipes whined as the water was turned on. She wondered how her mother stood the monotonous days at home, cleaning the thin flowered rug in the living room, dust-mopping the bedrooms, making beds, washing out the tub and the cracked white sink, then cooking in aluminum pots, washing dishes and scrubbing a sinkful of soaking pans. She thought of Amy looking through the window at the backyard, empty, because no one went outside much but her father when he smoked and sat in the swing. Oh I don't want that, Alice thought. She imagined city curbs and snow and heavy coats, brightly lighted streets, picture windows overlooking lighted up buildings, shiny lighted up stores.

"Alice," her mother called.

"Yes?" She could feel her forehead hot from her daydreams.

"Dewey's on the phone."

I didn't even hear it ring, she thought as she hurried along the hallway. It's all right, Dewey, she thought. I'm glad you're fired. Alice avoided her mother's eyes, took the phone, and pulled the cord just around the corner into Amy's bedroom. "Dewey," she said, excited, her voice blurred, her heart still racing.

"Dewey," she repeated when he didn't answer.

"What are you doing?" he asked softly.

"Nothing." She could tell the shyness in his voice. It's my fault, she thought.

"I've washed the car. What have you been doing?" he repeated.

"I've been getting ready. Can you come over?" If only she could make him listen.

"Why?"

Alice could tell he wanted to. He just wanted her to ask again. "I've got a surprise to tell you."

"What is it?"

"Come over and see," she said.

"What is it?"

"I can't tell you over the phone," she whispered.

"Is your mother there?"

"Yes. It doesn't matter. We can go outside."

"What is it?"

"I can't tell you over the phone."

"Tell me."

"Are you home?" Alice asked.

"What?"

"Are you packed?"

Alice hoped her mother didn't mention their fuss. "Where are you?"

"I'm home," Dewey lied.

Alice heard her mother in the hall and hoped she didn't come into the bedroom. "Please come over," she said.

"Okay," Dewey said.

"I'll be here," Alice said. "Bye." She hung up, and hugged her arm around herself. She massaged the top of her shoulder bone. It hurt. For the first time all day she felt like she thought she would before her wedding. It wasn't even about the wedding. It was about college. She held the phone on her lap, picked up the receiver and listened to the dial tone. I knew he'd call. She hung up, breathed deeply, her worries gone. She looked at her picture on the cedar chest. It was her favorite photo: she was in the fourth grade, had dimples and long curly blonde hair. She thought she was beautiful in that photograph. She wanted a little girl that would look just like that. And be as good as she had been. She didn't really want to change anything in her life.

"Who called?" Amy asked, pushing open the door. The telephone stopped the door halfway. "Is the phone in there?"

"I'm off," Alice said and put the phone back on the hall stand. "Do you need any help with the cake?"

"No. It's iced. Was that Dewey?"

Alice avoided her mother's eyes. Amy stood in the doorway. She spoke slowly, as she was embarrassed about what she had to say. Alice glanced into the bedroom and realized that sometime her mother had cleaned off the bed, too, and had neatly filled up a good-sized box. She wished Amy had left the things alone. "Did you clean up my room?" she asked.

"I cleaned off the bed because I had to change the sheets. Who called?"

"Dewey."

Amy only had to wrinkle her lips to make her whole face look disappointed.

"Do you have any more boxes?" Alice asked.

"Why the garage is filled with them. What size do you want?"

"I'll get it later," Alice said.

"Now that you're getting married," Amy said, "you've got to learn to be independent. You've got to make Dewey learn too. I know that both of you are old enough to get married."

"He's independent," Alice said. She didn't really think that he was. She walked into her bedroom and noticed that Amy had set out the window cleaner.

"Well what would Dewey think if you quit your job too?" Amy asked.

"What would Daddy say if you didn't clean house?" Alice asked. She had wanted to spend all day getting ready: making up her face, fixing her hair, checking to make certain her wedding suit was perfect. She felt the rollers on her head, but the hair was still wet. Her bedroom was cluttered with clothes and with things she thought belonged to the room but now had to be moved.

"He'd know that I was sick," Amy said. "Have you ever seen this house dirty?"

"I cleaned the windows last week," Alice said.

"I vacuumed yesterday, but I've already done it again today. Keeping house is a fulltime job."

Alice said nothing.

"I know you two will do what's right," Amy said. "Everyone makes mistakes. I know Dewey's a good boy. I'm glad you're marrying him. Both of you are dependable. Daddy's glad, too."

Alice wanted to mention college. She kept her lips tight together and she looked away when Amy smiled.

"Do you need something from the store?" Amy asked.

"No."

"I brought the window cleaner in to clean the mirror so you could see yourself better," Amy said. "I've already done it." She took the bottle and Alice heard her, in a minute, open the cabinet under the sink, and replace the bottle. Alice opened the blinds so she'd see Dewey's car, and heard Amy start the car, saw her back slowly from the drive and on her way to the grocery store.

She took the empty bottle of Desert Flower perfume that had sat on her dresser for as long as she could remember and dropped it into the paper lined waste basket. Then she threw away hairpins she never used, and lipstick too short to reach her lips, too far down in the tarnished lipstick tubes for her little finger to reach. She noticed that Amy had set the report cards on the dresser and not put them into the packed box. Alice turned through the identical cards--A's in every subject, six weeks after six weeks, semester average, for the entire four high school years. Once Mrs. Powell, who lived in the only brick house on the block, had looked at them and asked: "Hasn't Alice ever gotten a C in anything?" Amy had laughed, and Alice had been both proud and insulted. She thought of the dumb girls who made B's and C's, never paid attention, couldn't answer a question with the open book in front of them, and even if she had to be called a brain, she didn't want not to know where the answer was. She would have been embarrassed to be unable to answer the simple test questions or even worse, not to have her assignment when it was due. Still, the report cards weren't too thick a stack and she couldn't really remember any six week's work in particular. As if one were identical to the other and now only an unimportant mark to put away in some drawer.

When she had first known Dewey she had thought he was smart, but not like she was. He would miss questions or leave them unanswered because he hurried. During classes he talked and passed notes more than he listened. His A's, she thought, were weaker than hers and inevitably there would be a certain material or time in every course that Dewey would say he was totally confused and ask her what she thought about the material. He understood when she showed him, but she had

99

suspected that he had just as soon cheat as learn the difficult problems. Only after she knew him did she change her mind--and he changed his. She had known that he thought that she was smarter than he was. But after she loved him, she began to wonder, from what he said--things she'd never thought of and didn't want to think--for instance, that Miss Terry didn't herself know how to solve some of the algebra problems and only used a test key or that Miss Dixon preferred books that avoided description--that perhaps he was smarter than she'd given him credit for. She was sure he was as smart as she was and sometimes she admitted to herself that he was smarter, even though she then felt dumb, uncomfortable, unsure what to say to him and asked him to explain what he meant. She decided to leave the old report cards at home. She took them to the small red finished desk in the dining room. There was a corner whatnot shelf nearby and Alice paused to look at the glass objects--she hadn't noticed the shelf in years. Each tiny bowl and painted plaster animal was dusted clean and shone. She remembered buying her mother the pink boot vase with tiny gold painted eyelets. Amy had been thrilled and had put the vase on the top shelf just after she unwrapped it on her birthday.

Alice tugged the right hand desk drawer open. It was heavy with papers stuffed in brown envelopes and the drawer gave, only with a squeak and with pressure. She wasn't sure where to put the cards and finally stuck them deep in the drawer, her hand sliding past a manila expandable file. She felt the spiral of a small notebook, and decided to put the cards under the notebook. She hoped it would be unnoticed. She slipped out the small notebook and stuffed the cards to the bottom so that the other folders and the rubber band tied bank statements and business envelopes crowded above, hiding the cards. When she glanced at the notebook she saw her name across it.

Curious. She opened it up. She thought at first that it was a keepsake, too; the first page was dated 1950 when she was eight. She curiously scanned the neat columns in her mother's handwriting. She didn't remember the expenses, then, turning the pages she did remember: material for her first formal for eighth grade graduation, $8.00; a camera ($4.50) for Christmas, a $2 pair of red shoes Easter; $25 for two weeks at church camp; her FHA dues, $2.95 for a monopoly set on her birthday. She flipped several pages, looking for diary notes. There were only the neat columns of figures. She paused when she turned to the last entry and realized that only the day before, her mother had entered the cost of floral arrangements for their small wedding: $20. There were the costs of the engraved invitations she had had to argue for, the sheets her mother had given her at the neighborhood shower, the fabric for the just finished suit. I bought my own trousseau, Alice thought. Then she saw a note of $100 as wedding presents. There were two red lines at the bottom of the list and a total for all the years since she was eight. Nothing else.

Alice knew she wasn't supposed to see the book and she took back her report cards and laid them on top of the desk. She glanced out the dining room window to see if Amy was in sight. Then she stuffed the notebook into the drawer and safely closed it.

She wondered, as she walked into her bedroom, if she was supposed to repay all the money. She thought that her mother and father had secrets just as she did. She would never have believed that they wrote down her presents and clothes and even expenses when she was sick. She could not help catching a cold, or, as she remembered, the $15 the doctor charged when she slipped on her bicycle and had to have eight stitches in her leg.

She didn't see how Amy could have written down how much her presents cost. They were supposed to be presents, not debts. Alice hoped Dewey never found out.

XI. DEWEY VISITS DOTSY

He could see her get up from the sofa bed in the trailer living room; "Just a minute," she hollered, and thundered past the window. From the porch he could feel her heavy footsteps going to the bedroom. "What have you got on?" he asked, walked right in and peered down the hall at his grandmother.

"Well I've got on an old gown, smart alec. I'm looking for a robe."

Dewey sank into the armchair. "What were you doing?" He felt easy with her and he leaned back, his hands behind his head, his eyes on her rhinestone decorated telephone that needed dusting.

"I was taking a nap. It's too hot in this box to stay awake all afternoon. I sure am glad you came by."

He waited silently for her. He noted the yellow cups and saucers and plates she'd had as long as he could remember. She seldom used them, they were cheap, heavy dishes, bright and pretty that she kept in the cupboard. Beside them was a set of butterfly embossed glasses that he'd given her long before and she had saved them, afraid one might get broken. Usually she didn't care because she was generous, but if you bought her something that struck her fancy she kept it for years before she gave it to someone who liked it, too.

"Hurry up," he said.

She didn't wear slippers. Her big feet still had corns. He had bitten one once, crawled up to her foot hanging off the bed, and tried to clip off the corn on her toe with his sharp teeth. She had gone through the roof laughing, then said, "Lord, boy don't you know better than that? They'll grow on your teeth."

"What's your hurry?" she asked. "You don't get married until tonight. I had to slip off to get married." She sat on the sofa bed and switched the fan up one notch. She had found a pink nylon robe that reached to her toes. "I worked all day my wedding day. Mama watched me like a hawk, too."

He waited for her to mention the ring first and he wondered whether or not his mother had lied when she said that Dotsy wanted it back. She looked at him just as she had that morning,

103

pleased that he'd come over, ready to give him anything in the world that she could. "I was down at the store earlier," he said.

"I don't think Lucille likes her baby getting married," Dotsy said. "It makes her feel old."

"She doesn't care."

"She sure does. She told me this morning that she sure hated seeing you get married so young but there wasn't anything she could do about it. I think you surprised her."

"She told me she thought I should get married if that's what I want."

"Well it is."

Dewey meant that he knew Lucille was as glad to get rid of him as he was to go. She didn't have to say it. She told him by what she didn't say when they were alone: never the slightest objection to his leaving or until that day, a hint of a present. Around others she would squeal "Can you believe Dewey's getting married?" but privately she took him dead serious. He did, too. I'm getting married anyway, he sometimes thought, you can say you're glad. Lucille avoided the subject with him. She acted as if she had no opinion whatsoever, and had no intention of forming one. If he mentioned getting married, Lucille was uneasy, just as she was whenever he asked her for a favor. He never asked her directly what she thought about his getting married because his feelings were hurt. He knew for certain that she didn't mean the protests and surprises she expressed whenever she talked about it to others.

"She'll be glad to get rid of me," he said.

"Anyone would be the way you act. It nearly killed me when my baby married. I drove all the way to Louisiana and gave him a check for all but one hundred dollars I had in the bank. I didn't like his wife but I didn't say anything. She didn't even ask me to stay a week."

"I think I should get married," Dewey said.

"I think you should, too. Alice is shy, but she'll make you a good wife. You're out of school and old enough."

"I'm seventeen, I'll be eighteen in three months. Alice will be eighteen next February." He could see that his grandmother really did want him to do what he wanted. He thought again about the ring and decided to be honest about it. "If you want to keep the ring," Dewey said, "you can have it back. It's your ring."

"It's your ring," Dotsy said, "I'm not an Indian giver. Have I ever asked you for anything back? I said I'd give the ring to the first grandchild that got married--weren't you there when I said it?"

Dewey nodded.

"Lucille was too," Dotsy said. "She says she doesn't remember it, but she does. I sat right here and said I'd give it to the first grandchild that married. When he didn't want it, I was glad because I don't like his wife. I always hoped you'd have it, Dewey. I know that you and Alice will appreciate it."

"We will," Dewey said proudly.

"Mother never really wanted me to have it, but no one else wanted it then. It's solid gold." She brushed lint off the elbow of the pink robe. "Why couldn't Lucille admit to me that she was here?"

Dewey thought he knew but he didn't tell. He picked up an old framed photograph of his mother and her two sisters. His mother was the thinnest, with knobby knees and smiling buck teeth. Both his aunts kept their lips closed, and one was plump in the tight dress she had worn.

"Did you tell Mother you wanted the ring back?" he asked.

"What?" Dotsy asked.

"Mother said you wanted the ring back because Paula wants it."

"I never said I wanted the ring back, Dewey. If you don't want it, I'll keep it, but not for Paula. Maxine told me just a while ago that Paula wants a diamond ring when she gets married. I don't think she even knows whether or not she's going to marry Butch. If you don't want the ring, I'll keep it."

"I want it," he said, furious with his mother. "I just thought that you wished you hadn't given it to me."

Dotsy sighed. "If I'd wanted it back I wouldn't have given it to you in the first place."

Dewey suspected that maybe his grandmother had said something after all, but had changed her mind facing him. He couldn't tell from her expression. He didn't care now that he had the ring and he wanted doubly to show it to Alice that afternoon. "Alice and I both want the ring," he said. "We appreciate it."

"It's yours already," Dotsy said, "and anything else you two want that I can give you is, too." She rested both her palms on her knees, her robe looked tight about her neck chapped from her doing yardwork in the sun. She never had worn a bonnet since she had moved to Grand Prairie, but she kept her old red checkered one on a nail in her closet. Dewey had seen it and remembered the succession of summers he had spent with her and she had worn a bonnet whenever she went out into the hot sun, had kept her yard watered and green, profuse with flowers growing in cultivated beds with blooming plants hanging from the pots, and vines too thick with leaves to see the trellises they grew upon.

He wanted to tell her about the furniture and the raise. He wished he could tell her about Al, but he knew that the minute he left she would be on the phone, and he held back. He felt formal with her: a little less loving, disappointed. "Thank you," he said.

"Why there's no need to thank me."

"Did Mother really say she was looking for me?" He couldn't tell if she knew how he felt.

"Yes she did."

"Did she say why?"

"She wants you to come down to the store. You should— it's the last day you're her baby. Tomorrow you'll be married. You should go help her if she's busy and needs someone."

"Did she say anything else?" He knew she didn't need anyone else in the office. She only wanted to make up.

"No," Dotsy said. "What else is there to tell?" She opened her eyes wide.

He didn't want to feel cold toward her but he saw that she was prying. "Were you and Granddad married in Wichita?" he asked.

"Lord, no, you know better than that. We were married in Rising Star. We lived there five years before he had sense enough to move."

"Why did you move?"

"You're not fooling me one bit," Dotsy said. "You're just changing the subject. Lucille told me you had an argument with Al and said she was too embarrassed to show her face. It never hurts to ask for a raise, Bud, but you can't always expect to get one. And you sure don't argue with your boss over it, especially when he's been as good to you as Al has. Most stepfathers wouldn't even let you work for them."

Dewey would have argued with anyone else; with Dotsy he only thought how wrong she was and he looked up at the butterfly glasses to calm himself.

"Your mother only wants the best for you two. She thinks you're immature--she's worried. I had to annul her first marriage."

"You had to what?"

"When she married that red-haired boy--what was his name. Ronnie. She wasn't married but two days--when she was sixteen and ran off to Oklahoma with him."

"She never told me about it. She was married before she married Daddy?"

"Lord, don't mention it to her. I told her she wasn't going to marry him--he was good for nothing--spent all day at our place and wouldn't work--but she ran off with him anyway. She came back two days later and told me she didn't want to be married to him. I took her straight to the courthouse and never caught sight of him again."

"Who was he?"

"He was just some old boy who used to hang around the house. I don't know where she met him. Lord I remember he even had freckles on the palms of his hands. He was covered with them. I never did understand what she saw in him."

"Did she love him?"

"She said she did. She didn't know what love was. Don't you tell her I told; I thought you knew. I don't guess the truth hurts, though." She unbuttoned the neck of her robe and took off her bifocals to clean. "Now you don't tell I told. She didn't want you to know."

"She's been married three times then."

"Don't you tell," Dotsy said. She got up to fix him a glass of sweet iced tea, and she patted his shoulder as she passed him. "I sure do love you," she said.

There were, inside the curls of his perception, tiny compartments with doors he knocked upon to get into. Inside the new worlds, slight alterations of configurations thrilled him, but nothing more than a tickle. He felt sometimes like a tree with branches that never met, and he thought that if his thoughts never linked but were all one way, he would spend forever furnishing various things he believed in or felt. He could see to the end of his thinking, to rubber walls that made no noise when he beat against them. Once he had felt that the inside of his head would cave in at the touch of his fingers and he pressed against his skull, but he learned nothing. It was as if he had awakened, dissatisfied, outside of his life and could do nothing.

He was vaguely dissatisfied with everything as he left Dotsy's and drove toward Alice's. He could taste every experience of the day as a sour spot in his stomach. The events seemed as thick as saliva, bad medicine he had been forced to swallow. Nothing more than biology, as if he had dreamed them after eating onions or had thought them up hastily while he lay in bed with a cold. He wondered for a minute if he was crazy and the people that he saw walking along the sidewalk were sane and happily busy. They were no more than irritating faint tints at the ends of his vision. They disappeared into stores, got in and out of their automobiles, wore familiar expressions on their faces. He could see that none of them were any different from mirrors of his own reflection and he did not want to see them or hear them. He wanted something to etch into the bubble that had caught and floated off with him.

Silly, he told himself, feeling that in his fingertips was a certain power, his alone, to magnify the least sensation he had, to distort and refine the sensation until what he felt was unique, out of kilter, tailor-made to keep him happy in his individual life. As if everyone were being thrown together by the same power and fragilely separated by curving and turning the shape of the whole away from its own vision.

He put on sunglasses he kept on the dashboard and noticed the sun sparkle on the chrome strips that ran along the bulky front fenders. Alice could help him. When no one else could, she could, because she had a more objective point of view. She was, he thought, impeccable, not subject to the warped emotions he felt. He looked out the side window as he pulled up to a stoplight and smiled at the lady in the next lane. Guess what, he thought of telling her, I'm getting married and you know how important that is. The light changed; he pressed on the gas, then as he passed the A & P, switched to second, then third, and he felt calmer. He guessed he would go ahead and show Alice the ring. I wish we were already married, he thought. He switched stations on the radio and listened to the beat of the music.

He wondered what Ronnie was like and why his mother had run off with him. He could not imagine her loving anyone before his father. He sensed that she must have been wild, or at least ignorant, to run off with him. Probably it had been nothing more than something physical they both had wanted and his mother had not enjoyed. She must have wanted to leave home. He was curious why she never mentioned it. Perhaps there were a thousand things about her he would never know. He felt cold about them, as if he didn't care about knowing if she didn't want him to. He didn't care to pry into things about her he didn't want to know. He even felt sorry for her.

A cold attitude, he thought, just as she has toward me. He suspected for a minute that it came from a lack of love. That was exactly how he interpreted the confusing things she did: her insistence that he deliver at the store or sweep, when he was old enough to sell or work in the office. Why she made him and no one else clean up the restrooms it was impossible to get the stink out of. She had never come to him openly; told him frankly that she liked him or anything that he did—as if she really didn't, she complimented him behind his back and he heard secondhand that she was proud of his grades or had called him a hard worker. But she couldn't say something nice to his face because, he thought, that she didn't mean it. He even felt that she was jealous of him and only liked the things he did that she could tell her friends about and be complimented. She didn't like them herself. She would have preferred an entirely different son, certainly better looking. I'm glad I'm not, he thought, mad at her, and self-righteously thinking that some day she would see what was really important. Then he decided that she was right and that was exactly how he wanted to be but wasn't.

XII. LUCILLE AT WORK

Lucille hung up the phone and thought that her daughter sounded upset. Her kids weren't close like she was with her sisters. She told Joan that Dewey didn't want the children at the wedding, and she said that she didn't know why, either. Because he and Alice thought they were smart. She'd been having a time with Dewey--he really thought he was something just because he was getting married. Then she discussed what Joan should wear and she said the blue suit that hid most of the weight she'd gained in her hips, but Joan wanted to wear a tight black dress Lucille disliked. "Dewey told me to tell you not to wear that," Lucille said and was glad when Joan agreed, even if it did hurt Joan's feelings. Her feelings were hurt too easily; she cried at the drop of a hat without anyone knowing why. "Besides," Lucille had said, "your corsage is blue," and said, "Yes, he sure did buy you a corsage. Yes it was nice of him." Then Lucille dialed the florists and ordered a blue corsage for Joan and thought that good, she wouldn't be embarrassed at what Joan wore. She remembered when Joan used to be thin and pretty and could wear a tight dress and not look like a fat girl.

She hadn't sent the invitation to Don Junior yet, but he was in medical school in Ohio and didn't care anything about family anyway. I'll buy something for Dewey and Alice and put Don's name on it, she thought. She hated to buy anything because of how Dewey acted, especially after she'd offered him the furniture, but she didn't want anyone to know that Don Junior hadn't sent a present. She decided not to buy much--salt and pepper shakers would be just fine. If anyone asked, she'd say Don Junior sent her the money and she picked out the present herself. She laid the invitation in the outgoing stack of mail.

I wonder if Don's coming to the wedding, she thought. I don't mind if he comes; he should if he wants to. Whether or not Dewey wants him to. She had been dying her hair for over four years and she wondered if Don's curly hair was grey. She couldn't feature him grey-haired. She hoped he did come. Why don't I call and ask him, she thought. No one will know. Don has every right to come to his own son's wedding. She hesitated, knowing she'd be upset if Marge answered, then she thought: of course, I'll call him at work.

"I'll be back in just a minute," she told Bobbie, and took five dollars worth of change from the register. Outside, she slowed, feeling a little afraid of what Don might say.

She used the pay phone booth at the Town House restaurant two blocks away. She felt uneasy just to put the $1.75 in the change slots. Her chest was tight and she tapped her hands on the telephone book, looked at the cover she'd seen a hundred times, and held her breath as the phone rang. What's he going to think? she asked herself and switched the phone to her other ear. She hoped he wouldn't be angry with her, and her voice was barely audible when she asked for him.

"Yes?" he said when he came to the phone. His voice hadn't changed a bit.

Lucille giggled lightly. "Good morning," she said. She was as flattered as ever to talk with him. "It's me." She had never dared to call him at work when they were married.

Don said nothing.

"It's Lucille, Don."

"How are you?" he asked, his voice tense. She had hoped it would be. She felt so different talking to him, nervous, afraid--but glad. She could tell that he never expected her to call.

He couldn't control his voice--it wasn't smooth or peaceful; it was upset, like it had been those hundreds of afternoons they decided to separate because he was unhappy.

"I'm fine. Do you mind my calling you?"

"I'm glad you called," he said. "I wasn't doing anything but wasting time."

"I wasn't either," Lucille said.

"I guess you're calling about Dewey. Is he really getting married?"

"Isn't that awful?" she said. "I've told him not to."

"I don't guess you can stop him if he wants to. I'm going to send him some money this afternoon. I don't have much I can give him."

"They don't need money," Lucille said. "Dewey's got a good job at the store."

"I'll send him twenty dollars. How are you doing?"

"Just fine," Lucille said.

"I guess I would be too if I had a little more money. It's hard to raise a second family."

Lucille bit her lip just thinking about Don's other kids.

"That's too bad," Lucille said. "I'm glad they're yours and not mine."

"You don't know—you haven't had any other kids."

"I never wanted any," Lucille said.

"I've got to hang up now," Don said.

Lucille thought that he might. She realized that she had begun to sweat in the hot telephone booth. She made a face and decided he could if he wanted to. "I guess I shouldn't have called you," she said. "I just thought that you might want to come to your own son's wedding."

"I do want to."

"Then why don't you? You could drive here after work; the wedding isn't until eight."

"I will."

"You can come by the house first if you want to."

"I don't think I have time," he said. "I probably won't be alone. I'll try to come, though."

If she'll let you, Lucille thought. "Dewey's going to be embarrassed if you don't come," she said. "He's expecting you. . ."

"Well you're going. And Dewey can get married whether or not I'm there. You know that."

"I damn sure do."

"I'll try," Don said.

"Goodbye," Lucille said. "You don't want to go just because I'm going to be there."

"That's not true."

"Goodbye," Lucille said again and hung up. She opened the folding booth door and walked past the parked cars in front of the restaurant. She could see their store at the end of the broad alley and she decided to avoid the shops. She hoped Don came. She wondered what she should wear. Something new that would show him how nice she could still look. She walked over a yellowed letter stuck to hot tar in the alley. She had a letter that Marge had written Don when she and Don were still married. It was 13 pages long, scribbled over and over and over "I love you." Lucille had found it one day in Don's coat pocket. "Can you imagine?" she said to Dotsy when she showed her, and Dotsy had said, "You can bet Don read all 13 pages of it." Lucille tried to think what box of keepsakes she had hidden it in. I could give it to Marge tonight, she thought. It's hers, not mine.

She couldn't help but feel sorry for herself. She thought she'd been a fool again. Somehow Don could take away her confidence as if he knew every thought she had and what was wrong with it. Even so, she couldn't help wondering what he would have said if she hadn't hung up. She hurried, walking.

No matter what she did, he had always found fault. He was ashamed of how she dressed because she bought the cheapest clothes so he could wear nice ones to work. "Isn't she tacky?" Don said often, after he introduced her at a party. "I'm going to take her shopping," he'd say. He never did; he only complained when they met his friends. Otherwise, he told her that she spent too much money and he didn't know what he was going to do to make more.

But he was good-looking, and she did feel tacky around him. She never once thought that he wasn't smarter than she was because he could do all the things she could, faster, and criticize her. He was good about helping with the housework or with cooking on Sunday while she took the kids to church. He would have roast beef with boiled potatoes and carrots and often, he would have done the wash too and she would see the clothes flapping on the line. He went fishing Sundays and let them go, and she fished and kept the kids quiet so they wouldn't scare away the fish. Don picked a certain spot to fish from, cast out the line, and waited silently. If he changed spots he was quiet: he got angry if he heard anything but the plop of his sinker into the water and the low hum of his reel as he wound it. Some afternoons he caught nothing and was in a bad mood as they drove. If so, the kids couldn't talk in the car either; they sat by the windows, looked out, and thought to themselves.

Lucille thought he had a good personality because he could talk about any subject. People were always telling her, "Don sure is handsome–you'd better watch him," or "Don is about the smartest man I ever met." But she loved him because of how silly and thrilled she could feel when they were alone and talked, or if he put his arm around her as they listened to the radio or sat on the front porch. He called her "Honey" and he would hug her close like she was really the most wonderful thing in the world to him. She never blamed him for having a temper.

She wondered now, as she was crossing the street to the store, what her life would have been if Don had not left her for Marge. If they were still married in Wichita and she had never lived in Grand Prairie or met Al.

The sun made her forehead shine. Why on earth did Al turn down Dewey's raise? she thought. She had never thought for a second that he wouldn't agree. Lucille wanted to wring his neck for it. She went into the office and sat at her desk.

"Where is everyone?" she asked.

"No one has been in since you left. I'm doing the inventory."

"Has anyone called?"

"No one."

Lucille opened her purse and powdered her face with the rubber foam puff. Then she said, "I'm going across the street, I'll be back in a few minutes."

She hoped that Dayton's across the street still had the red dress she looked so good in when she tried it on. She waited for the red light to cross. I'll tell Dewey he can have his raise, she decided. Why would Al tell him no? It burned her up. Dewey was her last child. She felt hurt that Al didn't care.

She thought she'd buy the red because it looked good on her--she could tell and she would get her hair fixed and wear the heart necklace with diamonds that she had picked out for Al to buy her when they got married. She hurried, smiling, into the ladies' shop. Of course, she would give Dewey the raise. She thought of how pretty she wanted to look and she smiled, for the first time all day.

115

XIII. IN ALICE'S BACKYARD

Alice carefully brushed her hair and looked out the window whenever she heard a car pass. She wore light pink lipstick she had saved for her wedding. She closed her eyes, pressed the eyelash curler on her eyelashes, one side then the other, and sat, perfectly still, at the foot of her bed. She didn't want to muss herself. She was glad Amy had gone out for groceries. She could smell the sweet perfume she had bought to wear that night too, but already had dabbed behind her ears and on her wrists. The fragrance made her want to breathe in deeply, as nervous as she was. She looked at the white sunlight on the parched grass, the little oaks along the front curb; she was as still as a photograph.

She moved when she saw the convertible: first she felt her pulse, then, as she got up, she heard the jingle of her gold charm bracelet. She was on the front porch before he was and let him kiss her.

She felt pretty, smelling so good.

"You're all ready," he said.

"I just washed my hair," Alice said. "Come on in."

They walked into the small living room, and straight into the kitchen. "Come on," Dewey said, "lets go out back."

Alice hated to go into the sun.

Dewey sat in the chain swing that hung from a rusty iron frame. Alice stood beside him, a little shade across her face. She could see how upset he was.

"Sit here," he said, and she sat close beside him in the swing. Their knees touched. She pressed her hands against her skirt to keep them from trembling.

Dewey looked at her as he talked. "When I went to the store this morning, Mother gave me new furniture," he said. "She gave me a sofa and end tables and two lamps."

Alice didn't say anything.

"I was glad because we don't have any furniture."

Alice waited for him to go on. She understood that his telling her meant something and she was gladder than she could say when he took her hand. She wrapped her fingers tightly about his.

117

"She told me to ask Al for a raise. I didn't want to ask him; you know I wouldn't. But we needed more money, and Mother told me if I wanted the furniture that I had to ask."

"I don't care about the raise," Alice said.

"When I asked him, he asked me how long I'd worked at the store. He said I couldn't have a raise." Dewey looked away from her, his face angry. It seemed too simple. He glanced at Alice to see if she understood.

Alice thought to herself that it was good that all of it had happened. Right now, because nothing could be better than Dewey telling her what he thought, what upset him. She thought that yes, he was right. She had never understood his family before. She cuddled as he put his arm around her; she leaned her head against his shoulder. She wondered what his mother would say about their conversation and she told herself that she didn't care.

"I don't think I have a job," he said. "Mother wants me to apologize to Al. I'm not going to."

"Don't."

"I'm going to look for another job if you don't mind working at the draft board while I do. I'll find something. We can go ahead and marry."

"I've got four hundred dollars," Alice said. "I've been waiting to tell you because I didn't want us to count on it."

Dewey's smile showed her how glad he was. "If I were rich you'd love me a lot more, wouldn't you?" she asked.

"You are rich," he said, "if you've got four hundred dollars."

"I do. I've been saving since the fourth grade, and I've never taken a penny out that I've put in.

"I haven't saved anything," Dewey said.

"You spent it on me."

He thought that he had too, but he didn't regret it. He hugged Alice closer and told himself that once he was married, he would give her more than ever. He wished she'd say that she didn't care if he lost his job. I haven't really, he thought, you can say it. I can go to work tomorrow if you want me to. If I apologize.

Alice was ashamed to tell him about the notebook her parents kept. It was on the tip of her tongue and she looked at him, wanting so much to tell. She wondered if her mother would notice that the notebook had been moved and put back. "I found a notebook," she blurted out, her cheeks crimson.

He looked at her curiously, wondering what she meant.

"Mother doesn't know. She was at the grocery store and I found a notebook that lists everything they've spent on me since grade school--even presents." She immediately blushed and looked toward the garage out back.

"What do you mean?" Dewey asked.

"They've written down all the money they've had to spend on me."

"Why would they do that?"

"I don't know," Alice said. Her throat was as red as her face now. She thought her mother was back home. "I guess they want me to pay it back but I'm not going to."

Neither said a word. They shuffled, his arm wrapping her up, her head against his shoulder. He squeezed her hand gently; they listened, to the sound of a car far off, and Dewey looked at the sky, squinted and thought that his face was sweaty. He wished they could sit in the swing forever. I'll never love anyone but you, he thought; he wished he could do something particular to show her. He yawned. He hadn't realized how tired he felt. They rocked the swing slowly and he listened to squeaks of the chain links. He could see Alice's mother looking out the window at them, and he sat up.

"I can keep my job," he said. "Al didn't really fire me; he just wouldn't give me the raise. I don't want to work at the store anymore."

"Why don't we go away to college?" Alice faced him because she was afraid he would say no. "I can work and you can work part-time and go to school."

"What?" he asked.

"You're too smart not to go to college."

"I want us to," he said.

"I mean *now*."

"Let me think about it," he said, frowning. He thought definitely that she was right. He squinted his eyes, wiped his fingers across his forehead. He didn't want her to know what he was thinking. He closed his eyes, felt a dreamy happiness, and thought: it's over; we're going to get away. He figured that wherever they went on the money would be far enough, and he could work until September. In fact there was no reason why they both couldn't go to college. She could go part-time if he could. He didn't want to go if she didn't.

"Why not?" she asked.

He frowned, pretending to disagree.

"If you go, too," he said. "We can both go part-time."

"How can we both afford to?"

"I won't go if you don't. Don't you want to?"

"Of course I want to."

"Then we will," he said. "We'll both go and save money this summer."

For a minute Alice was afraid that he had suddenly changed his mind. "But I want to get married."

"We'll be married," he said. "Do you know where we're going to move to?"

Alice shook her head and hoped she'd like it. She could feel goosebumps on her arms.

"Tennessee."

She liked it. She'd never been there and wondered what it would be like. "I'm glad," she said.

"We drove through Tennessee once when we went to Washington, D.C. It's beautiful. We'll go to a small school in Tennessee."

She was more excited than she had been all day. As if she couldn't sit there any longer, had to get up, to look in the mirror, to think about her clothes, about anything else. "Can we go?" she asked.

"We're going," he said. "And we're going to college. Don't you want to?"

"Yes. I've always wanted to."

"We've just got to go on, then," he said. "No one here cares if we go to college or not."

"I want to see Tennessee."

"Then we'll go. Definitely." He held her hand tightly. He could see nothing but the charm bracelet on her thin wrist and her red skirt. "Don't you really want to?" he asked.

"Yes. Do you?"

"Of course."

"Can we afford to?"

"Yes."

He looked up the small tree branches toward the bright sky. He said nothing, then said, "I've always wanted to go to college." He wondered why he hadn't thought of it.

They jumped at the bang of the screen door. Alice's mother shook out a bathroom throw rug; she stood on the small porch, shook vigorously, her head turned. "What are you two doing?" she asked. "It's nearly four o'clock."

Neither of them had suspected it. Dewey didn't want to go. Then he thought of telling his mother and decided that she would still be at the store. He didn't want a raise or any of the furniture. "We'll go to Tennessee tonight," he said. "You'd better tell your parents."

Alice thought of what she had to do: packing, straightening, throwing old clothes away, telling her parents when her daddy came home. She wanted to privately look up Tennessee in the atlas.

He kissed her, then hurried off, out the gate and around the yard to the front. When Alice stood up, her heart beat even faster and she felt that everyone knew already and was thrilled as she was. She went into the kitchen, hummed to herself, and sat in a dinette chair.

"What did he want?" Amy asked.

Alice noticed the scarf over her mother's rolled up hair and a grimace, where her lips turned down, the dishrag in her hands as she wiped the kitchen sink, the empty grocery sack by the counter, ready for trash. She rubbed her back against the smooth plastic chairback and thought to herself that she was afraid because she was so happy.

XIV. THE PARENTS

Dewey wanted to tell his mother because he knew she wouldn't be expecting it. He was pleased with unsettling her. She wouldn't even be seeing more of him after that night. He walked past the new furniture in the store and he thought that he would not give in to the fuss she would put up. He was amazed that he could actually have cared about a sofa and lamps. Now he thought he'd feel depressed if he were stuck with them. He thought the less he had to carry with him, the better.

"Where have you been?" Lucille asked. "I've been calling all over town looking for you. Mother said you went by there." She sounded as if they were already late to the wedding.

Dewey nodded, then sat on the metal desk that Bobbie usually worked at. She had taken the deposit to the bank.

"I did."

"It didn't take you that long to drive here. Did you go by Alice's?"

"Yes."

"What did she say?"

"Nothing."

"Here," Lucille said and opened her purse. She quickly handed him a folded up bill. "That's your raise," she said.

Dewey handed the money back but she wouldn't take it. "I want you to have it," she said. "I don't appreciate your insulting Al, but I want you to have the raise for your wedding present."

He understood there was nothing to do but put the money in his pocket unless he wanted to argue.

"Have you packed?" She hurried to the back of the office and took the paper box from the sack. "Tell me if you like this. I bought it just for tonight." She took out the red dress that was thin and soft-looking and held it up at her shoulders.

"It looks nice."

"What should I wear with it?"

"I don't know," Dewey said. "It's pretty."

"I called your daddy," Lucille said. "He's coming too. It's not right for him not to come to your wedding."

"I don't mind."

"I don't care if he comes, but I thought I'd call him if you weren't going to."

Dewey smoothed his hand over the felt desk pad. "I wasn't," he said. He knew she wanted an excuse.

"Were you?"

"No, I wasn't."

"Then I'm glad I did. How do you think I'd feel if you didn't call me?"

"I would have called you," he said.

"Then you should have called him. He hasn't done much for you but he loved you."

"I went by Alice's." Dewey glanced at the clock and thought that he wanted to call Sue before anyone got home.

"What did she think, your going by there on your wedding day? She's trying to get ready."

"She was glad."

"What did you go by there for?"

"I wanted to talk with her about working at the store," he said.

"Why did you want to talk about that? We don't need her at the store."

"I mean me. I'm not going to work here anymore."

Lucille set down the letter opener in her hand and calmly turned toward him. "What are you going to do? Where can you get another job?"

He instantly realized that she was as glad as he was. He was the more surprised. "I'm going to college. We both are."

Lucille looked as if he hadn't said anything. "How?"

"We're going to Tennessee," he said. "We're both going to work and go to college at night." He considered telling her about Alice's $400 but he didn't. I can find a hundred jobs, he thought, whether or not you believe it.

"What did Alice's mother say?"

"Alice is going to tell her."

"I don't know what to tell you," Lucille said. "It's your business." She told herself to make sure to put back the inventory tags on the furniture she'd given them. She'd hidden them in her purse. "I guess if you've decided, you've decided."

"We've decided." He wanted to sound more positive than he felt. "We're going to go tonight after the wedding."

"Did you wash your car?" Lucille asked.

"No, but I'm going to."

"You wash it before the wedding. I'd be ashamed to get married in a dirty car."

"What do you think of it?" he asked.

"I think it's a good thing for you to do."

"You don't think we're too young?"

"You can apologize to Al and keep your job here. But you'll have to volunteer to work on Sundays if you want a raise."

"I did volunteer."

"You did not."

"I'm not staying anyway."

"Then why ask me?" Lucille said. "There's nothing I can do if you've made up your mind. If you're old enough to get married you're old enough to work where you want to."

"What do you think of Tennessee?"

"I don't know anything about it. I've never been there."

"We drove through when we went to Washington, D.C.," Dewey said.

"That was a long time ago. I don't think we went through Tennessee, did we?"

"Yes, we did."

"No, we went through North Carolina."

"We went through both of them."

"Well I don't remember. Don't ask me if I'm so stupid."

"I liked it," Dewey said.

"I wouldn't want to live there. I wouldn't live anywhere but Grand Prairie." She snapped her purse shut and dusted off the desk with an old kleenex. "I wonder what shoes I should wear? Do you really think the dress is pretty?"

"It's real pretty."

"I don't want your daddy to think I look flashy."

"It doesn't look flashy."

"Well, I wish Al would hurry. I'm ready to go home."

Dewey had known the store for years; worked there afternoons, every summer, and it was where Lucille was whenever he called her for something. "I'll be home," he said. "I'd better hurry."

"You wash the car."

"I already have," he said.

"Do you really want to go away? You don't have to if you don't want to. You have a good job here. You can work some in the office."

"I want to go to college," he said. He felt his hands shaking as he walked out, along the rows of furniture, and listened to the bell jangle as he opened the door and was suddenly outside in the heat.

Dewey made sure no one was in the house, then he took the phone into the bedroom and closed the door. He hoped Sue and not her mother answered. He thought that he should hang up if her mother answered and he thought: suppose she's told. The phone rang once, twice, three times, and he looked out the window to see if Sue was next door, when someone picked up the receiver.

"Hello," he said.

"Hello." It was clearly her mother.

"She's in her bedroom, who is calling?"

"Dewey," he said uneasily.

"Just a minute."

He was relieved she didn't ask him anything else. He wanted to kiss Sue when he heard her voice.

"Is this Dewey?" she asked.

"Yes."

"Why did you tell Mother? Now she'll want to know why you called."

"She asked."

"She would."

"Where were you?"

"I was sleeping," she said.

He could tell by her voice that she was upset. He wanted to promise her that nothing was wrong, that if she waited, she

126

would find someone she loved more than him. "Are you upset about this afternoon?"

"No."

"You shouldn't be." He realized that he was and he reminded himself to check that the bed was okay. "I'm glad."

"I am too."

"We're just worried that someone will find out. No one will."

"No."

He prayed quickly, silently, that she was not pregnant and he thought that if God would let him by this one more time, just let him live safely through what he'd done wrong, let him marry Alice and no one know, then he'd not complain what happened to him. He wanted exactly what he had. Alice's love, their sudden freedom from everyone, the excitement of some place new. He wanted his arm around Alice and them driving, in the dark, some place neither had been or ever thought of going. Please God, he said to himself, forgive me once more. Don't let me die yet.

He still loved Sue sweetly, because she loved him and had given herself to him and he wanted her to be as satisfied as he was. At least he did like her very much and he didn't want to worry or have her worry. He wished she hadn't come anywhere close to his window. He wished he'd let her walk on along the street: he could hardly remember the pleasure he had had, as if it were only hers, or neither of theirs. "How do you feel?"

"Aren't you getting married at eight?" she asked.

"Yes."

"I don't think Alice would appreciate your calling me. Why don't you call her?"

"Because I want to talk to you. Alice and I are going to move to Tennessee."

"When?"

"Tonight."

"You don't have my wedding present," Sue said.

"We've already talked about it."

"I'll send it."

127

"Have you changed your mind about this afternoon?" He could feel her mind change back as he asked, because he cared enough to ask. "I don't want to say goodbye to you."

"You don't have to go."

"Yes I do."

"Mother's trying to listen," Sue said loudly, to frighten her mother away. "Why do you have to?"

"Because we're both going to work and go to college–and that's what you should do, too."

"You should," she said. "I'm glad you're going to college."

"Sue," Dewey said.

"There's nothing I can do about how you feel. If you loved me, you wouldn't marry Alice."

"That's not true."

"Yes it is."

"It's not."

"But I don't care like I did. I don't feel the same about you."

"What do you mean?" Dewey asked. "I haven't done anything to change your mind."

"No, I have. I've been thinking. I don't want you to write me or ever call me again. I was wrong about you."

"You weren't. You were wrong about life."

"No, about you."

"What about me?"

"You're not really nice like I thought you were," Sue said. "I've got to hang up. Our calls are limited to five minutes."

"Can I call you back?"

"No."

"Can I tell you something?"

"Yes," she said.

"I do love you," he said quietly and felt very much that he did and he was sorry that he did.

"Goodbye," Sue said.

He held the receiver after she hung up and he thought that it was broken off and he would have to think about it. He wanted to think about it. He wanted to decide what had happened, he was glad he told her he loved her. She was gone--

the first thing he'd lost in Grand Prairie that night, and he noticed the clock, and remembered he needed to get his old suitcase from the garage. He couldn't help but ask himself if she was right, and he thought that she was and he was not nice or he would not have taken advantage of her. I wouldn't have done it if I had known she really cared, he thought. I don't want her thinking I'm not nice.

"Dewey," Dotsy yelled from the front door as she walked in.

He went into the living room and saw his grandmother and his aunt Maxine. "Mother's not home yet," he said.

"We know that. We just talked to her over the phone. Sit down, we want to talk to you."

"I've got to pack," he said.

"That's just what we want to talk to you about. Sit down here," Dotsy said, "sit on my lap."

It was dim in the room with the curtains shut, and Maxine turned on the lights. Dewey sat on the floor and looked up at them sitting on the soft foam sofa. "I thought you two were fussing," he said.

"Well aren't you smart," Dotsy said. "For your information, Maxine and I don't fuss. What is this we hear about you moving out of town."

Dewey wondered where Paula was. He had hardly ever seen Maxine without her daughter. I guess Paula's the only one angry now, he thought. "Yes," he said.

"What do you mean 'yes'? Are you moving or not?"

"We're moving."

"I sure would hate to act so proud of it. You don't move away from your family because you want to. You only do it when you have to, if you love your family."

"I don't want to move away from you," Maxine said. "I don't appreciate your not bringing Alice by to meet me, but I'm willing to accept her as one of the family because she's your wife."

"I'm not moving away from anyone," he said. "I'm going to college."

"Lucille said you were moving to North Carolina."

"Alice and I are going to Tennessee and we're going to college."

"You can go right here."

"I don't want to go right here," he said.

"I remember your telling me when you and granddad left home."

"We didn't move but twenty-five miles and it was a mistake. We should have gone to the other side of the earth. But you don't have the problems that we had. Papa said he would shoot Max if I married him. There's no one I know of that's going to shoot you."

"I'm glad you're marrying Alice," Maxine said. "I just don't appreciate your not bringing her by to meet me. Lucille said she didn't blame me one bit. Paula took Butch by to meet her."

"She sure did," Dotsy said. "Maybe Dewey's ashamed of Alice."

"I'm not ashamed of her."

"I don't care if she's pretty or not," Maxine said.

"She is pretty!" Dewey lay back on the floor and felt irritated they were making him angry.

"How do I know if I haven't seen her? You should have brought her by."

"I will," he said.

"Not if you move to Tennessee."

"You'll see her at the wedding."

"Isn't that something? I'm not even going to the wedding because you haven't brought her by. I don't think you should leave tonight–your mother is taking it so hard. I feel sorry for Lucille."

"She doesn't care. She told me it was a good idea."

"I don't believe that," Dotsy said. She was upset when she was talking to me. She called from the cleaners just a minute ago. I'd hate to make my mother so unhappy on my wedding day. What do Alice's parents say?"

"They think it's fine," Dewey said. "They want both of us to go to college."

"I do too, but I don't think you should ever leave your family if you don't have to." Maxine slipped off her shoes and settled back, comfortable. "What would you do, boy, if you never saw your mother again?"

"I'd hate to say that, Maxine," Dotsy said. "But it's true. You only have one mother, Bud. She's yours whether you're happy with her or not."

Dewey said nothing. He squinted, looking at them on the sofa with the bright light on their hair. Dotsy was barefoot and Maxine wore a colorful schmoo dress that hid her stockiness. Her hair was short and messy and she wore sunglasses with white frames decorated with rhinestones. Dotsy wore a blue dress and gold wire glasses that hooked around her ears. He could see the gold through her grey hair. He sat a moment and watched them, then he wished that he could be alone again, or with Sue in the house and them gone and only him and Sue in the darkness, the quiet.

He wanted to tell them that he was sorry but he loved them and he was ashamed of them, not Alice, because of what they said to him and to each other. "I don't believe you," he said.

"Don't believe what?" Maxine was already stiffened.

"That you care whether or not I go. I wouldn't care if you moved back to Arizona. It's your business."

"Do you mean that?"

"If you mean me, then I don't care if you fry in Hell," Maxine said. "I just feel sorry for Lucille." She got right up, picked up her shoes, looked angrily around the room and stormed out the screen door.

"Now why did you do that?" Dotsy said. "You know what she's like. She only hoped you'd stay just like I do. Because I love you."

"I'm not leaving you," he said.

"I know that. And I wish the best in the world for you and Alice. I hope you do go to college and everything you want comes true. If Lucille is upset, she'll get over it."

"She's not really upset," he said.

Dotsy kissed and hugged him and he smelled her perfume and felt her heavy arms and kissed her back on the cheek, before she hurried after Maxine.

Then Dewey went into the garage and opened the garage door so he could have some light to find the old suitcase.

Alice sat absolutely silent in her bedroom with the door closed. She turned through an atlas she had bought in the fifth grade. When she found Tennessee, she nervously turned her back on the door. She studied the page. It was colored light orange and she read the name of every city printed on the map. She listened for her mother. She was stunned at how much had happened since she decided Dewey should go to college. Now she was going, as well, to a school she didn't know yet and in, of all places, Tennessee. She liked the Indian name. She bet Dewey would choose some curious spot they would both love. She liked the names of the cities and towns: Memphis, Cumberland, Chattanooga. She thought Nashville sounded like a city of Nashes. She hoped he picked some beautiful small town he remembered when he had been there. He had been to Tennessee twice: once when they drove across to Washington, D.C., and then when they drove back from Washington, D.C. to Texas.

She wanted to go to college more than anything after she wanted to get married. She thought she'd make all A's. And she began to think what she could major in and decided that English was her best subject. She had always thought she would make a good, strict teacher. She wondered if she should carry her report cards with her, but she decided not to. She could tell already that just she and Dewey would do the right thing.

Alice took the plastic rickshaw off the whatnot shelf and stuck it under a folded up dress in her suitcase, too. She knew that Dewey would think she was sentimental, but it was part of her room. She put in her Bible too, and felt better.

She had to rethink everything she was going to pack. Her clothes were scattered about the room. She couldn't decide what she should take. She filled the suitcase that had the plastic rickshaw first, then she carefully folded all the clothes-- those she would take and wouldn't: in a matter of hours she would be married to Dewey and on her way to Tennessee. She tucked her bankbook deep in her purse, closed the purse and put it into the dresser drawer. She heard the front door open: her father was home and she would have to tell them. Now, before supper even, as soon as he had changed his shirt.

She sat on the sofa when her father took his usual chair. He had changed shirts and shoes, and he held the folded newspaper to read. "So you're getting married," he said, and

132

chuckled, nodding his head in agreement with himself. "What time are you getting married?"

"At eight."

"Oh." He nodded again, slowly, saying nothing but grinning.

Alice was always irritated when he pretended not to know the simplest things she had told him a hundred times.

"At the First Baptist?"

"Yes, Daddy."

He nodded again, and smiled, his thick cheeks spreading. "Well, everyone gets nervous," he said.

She thought of the book with her name on it and she thought, I forgive you if you'll only try to understand me. She looked at the closed front door and the unpainted handle. There was a fly on the handle. She could see its spread wings and the tiny luminous eyes. She glanced at her father reading and felt guilty.

She knew that neither of her parents would approve of her leaving town.

"Have you finished packing?" Amy asked, coming in from the small kitchen. "Are you two ready for supper? Jonathan's not back yet."

"She's just talking with me," her daddy said proudly.

Amy sat in the chair beside his, across a small lamp table, and she wiped her wet hands on her apron.

Alice could tell from her mother's face that Amy understood that she was upset. She knew her parents thought that the problem was marrying and leaving home, and she felt angry at them.

"At eight, hmmm?" Ed said.

"I told you that, Daddy."

"We have to leave in an hour. Have you finished packing?"

"Just about," Alice said, her face pale.

Then no one spoke. Her father unfolded the newspaper. Alice blushed, wishing they'd ask her what she had to say. But Amy looked away from her, too, and watched out the window for Jonathan.

"Dewey and I are going to college," Alice said. Her throat was white and flushed. She made a red mark along it with her finger.

"You two should. You're about as smart as two people can be," Amy said.

"When you get the opportunity, you should go. I would have gone if I could have," Ed said.

"We're going now--we're moving to Tennessee."

"Tennessee?" Amy crooked her arm at her waist. "You don't know anything about Tennessee."

"Dewey's been there."

"What about his job in Grand Prairie?"

"We'll both work and go to school."

"It won't work," Ed said. "It just sounds good."

"Why are you going to work?" Amy asked.

"I've been working at the draft board."

"But you're not married. When you're married you'll have a house to keep and a family."

"You never have been to Tennessee," Ed said.

"Dewey has."

"But you haven't."

"No, I haven't."

"Then how do you know you want to go there?"

"Because Dewey does."

"That Dewey!" Ed chuckled and folded up the newspaper. "I thought he was more mature than that."

"He is."

"Then why is he doing it?"

"He's mature, Daddy. We both are."

"No one said you weren't mature, Alice," Amy said. "There's no need in crying."

"I'm not." But she was.

"I don't think Dewey's car would even make it to Tennessee," Ed said. "I sure thought he was smarter than that. If he wants to run off, I'm not sure he's ready to get married, though."

Alice looked at him furiously, thinking she would die if Dewey left her.

"When are you going?" Amy asked.

"Tonight."

"Tonight? Why you aren't packed to move. It gets cold in Tennessee in the winter. Your wool clothes are in the garage."

"I know it."

"People who run off when they have a responsibility usually always--almost always--never quit running. I'm talking from experience, from the guys I've seen start work with me and quit and think they're going to get something better. They never do. They wind up going from one job that looks good to another and pretty soon they can't find work. I'm surprised at Dewey. College is a lot harder than you think, too."

"I'm going to work, Daddy."

"What about when you have a kid and can't work?"

"I don't say you won't go to college," Amy said. "But life's a lot harder than you think at your age."

"You can't tell what's going to happen," Ed said. "But I didn't take him for that kind of a guy. I bet his parents won't let him go."

"For what kind of guy?" Alice asked.

"You've got to be careful who you marry Alice. You shouldn't marry someone who can talk you into something you know better than. He's not dumb--he's smart--but he's immature."

"I don't think so."

"I've seen it time and time again," Ed said. "But you can't learn from advice if you're too much in love with him."

I do love him, Alice thought. "I don't think you know him," she said. "I wouldn't marry anyone who was going to do something wrong."

"No, I don't believe you would," Ed said. "Maybe I'm wrong. I hope I am."

"We like Dewey," Amy said. "I never meant you shouldn't marry him. I bet when he talks to his parents he changes his mind. They're not going to let him go to Tennessee."

"You're right," Ed said. "I think your absolutely right."

XV. THE WEDDING

Dewey carried the boxes, still cool from the refrigerator, into the church and handed Dotsy the one marked "D." "Here," he said and gave Lucille hers too. She had especially ordered a white orchid.

"Where's Joan's?" Lucille asked. "Did the florist forget hers?"

"She won't notice." Dotsy smelled of heavy perfume and dusting powder. She had dressed up, to the teeth, but quickly, and wore colorful artificial flowers, imitation pearls, a dark straw hat with lilacs. "Any color is fine for me," she said. "I look like a garden; I ought to take these artificial ones off." She laughed, then whispered into Dewey's ear.

"Oh?" Dewey said, blushing.

"What's that?" Lucille asked.

"Daddy's here," he said.

"Shhh. He's waiting down the hall for Dewey. I told Dewey to look in and say something."

"Oh, Don isn't here, is he?" Lucille asked. She glanced around her. "Where is he?"

"He sure is," Dotsy said. "I noticed him the minute I got here. Maxine isn't coming and I rode with the Moody's. He looked lost too until he saw me. Don and I always did get along okay, Lucille. His face lit up like a candle when he saw me. I told him I'd send Dewey in as soon as he got here."

"Is Alice here?" Dewey asked.

"Aren't you going to go?" Dotsy pointed her finger to Room 103. The door was shut.

Dewey looked at Lucille to decide if he should. He wouldn't go if she didn't want him to.

"Well go on," Lucille said.

"Isn't he nervous?" Dotsy said.

Dewey walked red-cheeked past the chapel doors. He didn't look back and avoided the audience: he could see heads turning along the aisle. He looked at the door number again before he went in. He wished Dotsy would leave things alone.

"There's Alice," Lucille said. "She's not even ready yet."

Alice hurried into the side entrance. She carried a clothes bag and her hair was rolled up in curlers. Lucille waved hello to Amy who hurried after Alice to help her dress. Her little brother hurried too, and her father, each carrying a box.

"I'm surprised Don came," Lucille said. "He didn't send a present--his own son's wedding."

"He still looks like a million dollars. Dressed up and distinguished grey hair. I would have recognized him anywhere. He kissed me like he always did. I told him it'd be fine to talk with Dewey before the wedding if he wanted to."

"I'd like to see him," Lucille said.

"You won't be able to miss him. He sure is good-looking. So is that little girl of his."

Lucille stiffened. She thought how cold Don could be. She pinned on the orchid she held, trying not to muss the large bloom.

"I don't think he should have brought her here," Dotsy said.

Lucille didn't answer. "Does this look okay with this dress?"

"That's new isn't it?" Dotsy touched the soft material. "I've never seen red chiffon before. It's beautiful."

"Is it too much?"

"No, it isn't. I didn't dress up like you did, though."

"Maxine didn't come?"

"She got her feelings hurt and I don't blame her. But she didn't tell me until I called, wondering why she didn't come by. I had to ask the Moodys for a ride. There she is Lucille."

Lucille glanced at the small blonde girl leaving the chapel and going toward the water fountain. "I don't think she's so pretty," she said.

"I don't either," Dotsy said. "I don't know why people say she is."

"Was Dewey rude to Maxine?"

"He just told her that he and Alice both wanted to go. Maxine took it personally. She thinks everyone should be like Paula and not leave home."

Lucille felt embarrassed Dewey wanted to go. She wished he'd keep his mouth shut. It hurt her feelings too and she wondered if she should say something to him when he came out. "Why he'll be back," she said. "You know Dewey won't be able to stay away long. He doesn't know anything but Grand Prairie. He's just got big ideas."

Dotsy touched her on the arm as Julie darted back into the chapel. "She's kind of cute," she said, "but she's not beautiful."

"She sure isn't."

"He must be proud of her to bring her to the wedding. He introduced her to me like she was the prettiest thing in the world."

"He shouldn't have brought her," Lucille said. She couldn't help but make a face as she looked at Dotsy. Dotsy caught it and shook her head. "I guess Don was afraid to come alone," she said. "He knows he made a mistake when he left his family."

Dewey wasn't surprised at his father's expression: the eyes welled up, his face colored with emotion, contrasting with the white suit he wore. He was afraid his father would cry. He thought of nights years and years before when his parents would argue and he would end up having to sleep with his father who tried to tell him his side and argued against Lucille. Those were restless nights he had had to spend with Don, smelling the cigarettes he smoked, unwilling to listen to his apologies for their argument, and he understood then that he could not trust his father. The next night was as likely as not to end up in a similar fuss and Don would protest again that none of it was his fault.

Dewey felt a detachment he didn't understand as he looked at his own father. He thought he looked flashy in the white suit, his black shoes glowing with polish, and a fancy gold watch Don looked at as Dewey came in. Well what are you doing here? Dewey thought, as if he were only more trouble. If Don had sent birthday cards and Christmas gifts, if he had called--or written--but he hadn't, and seeing him face to face now, on such an important night in his life had little to do with what he wanted.

He stood still while his daddy kissed him.

Don stood back then, his face aglow, his eyes red. "I know you're nervous," Don said. "But I wanted to see you because I have to drive back tonight immediately after the wedding."

He shook his head as if he were surprised how Dewey had grown up.

When Dewey was ten, Don would come by certain Saturdays and take him swimming. Don drove a black Studebaker, waxed and neat as a pin. After swimming they would eat hot dogs at a diner. Dewey still remembered what Don once said: "Hot dogs. I wouldn't be eating hot dogs if your mother had listened to reason." And Dewey had tuned him out because he didn't want to hear any more about it from either of them. But he liked the chili dog and covered it with spicy mustard. After a year Don took him nowhere, and when they moved out of town, Don neither visited nor wrote.

"I wanted to see you," Don said again.

"Have you seen Alice? I'd like for her to meet you."

"No," Don said. "I'll see her during the wedding. I wish you could meet your sister Julie. She sure is pretty-- she'll be sitting with me. Look for her."

Dewey curiously noticed his father's hook nose and wondered why his mother or anyone else had said that he was good-looking. He didn't think so: he thought he'd like to tell him too, because his father was too dressed up, like Dotsy.

"I've changed jobs," Don said. "It's the same sales work, just another company." He shook his head. "I don't make much."

"We're going to Tennessee, " Dewey said. He could tell from the bulletin board that they were in an adult Sunday School class. "We're both going to college."

"I've never been to Tennessee," Don said. "I guess I know Lampasas too well to ever leave."

Dewey was glad Lucille had moved them to Grand Prairie and he was glad she married again.

"I saw Dotsy; she hasn't changed."

"No."

"She couldn't wait to get me alone. She told me you and Alice were leaving because you were mad at your mother."

"That's not true."

"You want to get away and I don't blame you. You shouldn't live around them."

"I don't want to get away," Dewey said. "Alice and I just want to go to college."

"Well I hope you do. I should have when I had the chance after the war."

Dewey nodded.

"I wasn't sure I should come until your mother called and said you wanted me to. I know she still has hard feelings about us."

"I don't think so," Dewey said.

"You make sure to write me your address when you're in Tennessee."

Dewey nodded.

"Here's forty dollars. I wish I could give you more."

"Thanks," Dewey said. He shook hands with his father and waited in the quiet room for his father to walk along the hall and into the chapel.

Lucille hurried into the room, her powder obvious in the bright lighting. "Can you believe how old he looks?" she said. "He looks like an old man."

Dewey hadn't thought Don looked different, but his hair was grey. Dewey thought then that he'd avoided his father's gaze.

"He hardly spoke to me," Lucille said. "I just saw him in the hall. I think he would have passed by without saying a word if I hadn't spoken to him first. I wouldn't have recognized him if I hadn't known who it was. Would you?"

"I don't think he's changed much." He wished she wouldn't talk about it.

"He sure has. He used to be good-looking. He hardly looks like the same person. What did he say to you?"

"Nothing much."

"He must have said something. You were in here fifteen minutes. Did he mention Julie?"

"No."

"Can you believe he brought her?"

"Did he?" Dewey asked.

"You know how that'll make your sister feel."

"Yes."

"I'm surprised he even came," Lucille said.

"He gave me forty dollars," Dewey said.

"He looked like he was about to cry. Like he did at Joan's wedding."

"I hope he doesn't," Dewey said.

"I do too. He's too old to cry like that. Do I look that old? Tell me if I do. I want to know."

"You don't."

"I bet I do, don't I?" She opened her purse for lipstick.

"No."

"Why he's an old man." She smeared the red lipstick on her lips. "I don't think I look that old."

"You don't. I'm surprised he came," Dewey said. "He didn't have anything to say to me. He said he was working for another insurance company but isn't making much money."

Dewey thought Lucille looked good in the red dress. Better than she had in a long time. Dewey bet his father was envious, maybe even sorry when he saw her. He thought his daddy should have been.

"He's probably not," she said. "He never did make much. Did you tell him you and Alice were leaving?"

"He doesn't have time to meet Alice," Dewey said. "He has to get back."

"Because his wife is probably waiting in Dallas. She has a sister there."

"I don't care," Dewey said. "He doesn't have to meet her."

Lucille glanced into her purse mirror and wiped lipstick from a front tooth. "Alice looks pretty," she said. "She just came in with her family. She isn't ready yet."

"Have you talked to her parents?"

Lucille moved closer to him. She took the white envelope with the two hundred dollars from her purse. "They look like it's okay with them if you move," she said. "Here, I want to give you this."

"Thank you," Dewey said and slipped it into his suit pocket without looking at the amount.

"If you need more, write me."

Dewey nodded.

"Don't mention it to Al."

He didn't even nod.

"Why don't you stay a few days and tell everyone bye?" Lucille asked. "You can stay with us; we won't bother you. You can take Alice by to meet Maxine. Everyone would like it."

Dewey walked to the window and looked at the dark parking lot. "We have to get jobs," he said. He felt prosperous with the envelope and the forty dollars.

"You'd better hurry," Dotsy said, bustling into the room, a blur of colors. "My Lord, your tie's crooked, boy." She straightened it, and put her arms around him.

Lucille stood near the door. "Why are you crying?" she asked Dotsy. "He's not going to leave yet. Don't cry; you'll embarrass him."

"I love you," Dotsy whispered in his ear and she hugged him tight, then let go, and wiped her eyes with a lace handkerchief she'd brought.

Alice could feel every eye on her as she walked down the aisle; she looked at no one. The white stephanotis and net scratched her wrist. She was every inch made up, her lipstick as smooth as ice, her hair shiny from spray, her skin more pale in the chapel light. She thought her suit was beautiful, and when she saw Dewey already at the front of the church, she could hear her skirt rustle and felt her heart beat because she had to walk so slowly. She could tell how embarrassed he was. She blushed, her hands turned cold, and for no reason she could think of, she wanted to cry as if she were empty.

She thought Dewey looked handsome. They had never both been embarrassed before and she caught him smiling, and she suddenly smiled, and they were both uneasy. She didn't care if her parents wouldn't approve of going to Tennessee. They hadn't said a word from the house to the church; only her little brother had and he didn't know she was going. She was glad Dewey still wanted to go. She listened to the preacher and she thought that Tennessee sounded wonderful. Her mother and father hadn't even gone anywhere for a trip but to Arkansas where they visited relatives. She was hurt they didn't care. She hoped Dewey hadn't seen her go into the church when she had her hair rolled up. She glanced at him again; he was listening to the preacher. I'm so happy, she thought, and I'm going to be happy for the rest of my life. She realized that she felt afraid, not empty.

Silly little ideas popped into her head about their future. She was thrilled both of them were going to college. Maybe they could graduate together.

"I do," she said, and pressed her foot on the carpet.

Dewey kissed her quickly and whispered, "Let's hurry." He didn't smile when he saw his father, red-eyed, like an eagle, and blowing his nose. He saw his sister dressed in a blue dress and she was crying, too. Dotsy sat beside Maxine, at the rear, and Maxine hadn't dressed up; she must have changed her mind and decided to come at the last minute; she wore the same muu-muu from earlier, and she was crying too, a smile on her thin lips. He didn't see Alice's parents.

Lucille was next out the chapel door after him and Alice. She kissed them both, while they walked to the side entrance where his car was parked. "You're going to the reception, aren't you?" she asked.

"Yes," Dewey said. "We'll be there in a few minutes."

"Don't be too late."

"We won't."

He unlocked the door for Alice, and noticed the white shoe polish scrawled on his convertible. "JUST MARRIED" was written on each door and across the trunk. He pulled off the tin cans tied with strings onto the back bumper, and he got in before many others crowded at the church door to watch. Alice scooted next to him. He changed gears, and out of the parking lot, put his arm around her as he drove straight along Main.

The excitement spread to the line of cars in the street traffic. Dewey ignored the people in the cars. He turned at the light, in the opposite direction of the restaurant where the reception would be. "We'll be late," he said.

Alice hugged close and said nothing.

Dewey was glad the ceremony was over. He didn't speak for a minute, either. He could think of nothing to say because he felt so happy, as if the car was candy, like Alice, soft and sweet and lovely. He thought he understood how she felt because he felt so wonderful. He had never been so excited.

They drove, silent and pressed against each other, the streets dark and houses lighted. He thought about Alice, about his mother busy at the reception. He knew she thought his father would come. He smiled to himself and thought of going to college. Alice sat beneath his arm and occasionally dabbed at her eyes with a kleenex. She wished they'd hurry and she was glad, when he finally started to the restaurant, because she wanted to be on the way to Tennessee.